Acting Edition

Corsicana

by Will Arbery

Copyright © 2023 by Will Arbery

"Come Clean"
Words and Music by Kara DioGuardi and John Shanks
Copyright © 2003 BMG Bumblebee and Sony Music Publishing (US) LLC
All Rights for BMG Bumblebee Administered by
BMG Rights Management (US) LLC
All Rights for Sony Music Publishing (US) LLC Administered by
Sony Music Publishing (US) LLC,
424 Church Street, Suite 1200, Nashville, TN 37219
All Rights Reserved. Used by Permission.
Reprinted by Permission of Hal Leonard LLC

CORSICANA is fully protected under the copyright laws of the United States of America, the British Commonwealth, including Canada, and all member countries of the Berne Convention for the Protection of Literary and Artistic Works, the Universal Copyright Convention, and/or the World Trade Organization conforming to the Agreement on Trade Related Aspects of Intellectual Property Rights. All rights, including professional and amateur stage productions, recitation, lecturing, public reading, motion picture, radio broadcasting, television, online/digital production, and the rights of translation into foreign languages are strictly reserved.

ISBN 978-0-573-71065-0

www.concordtheatricals.com
www.concordtheatricals.co.uk

FOR PRODUCTION INQUIRIES

UNITED STATES AND CANADA
info@concordtheatricals.com
1-866-979-0447

UNITED KINGDOM AND EUROPE
licensing@concordtheatricals.co.uk
020-7054-7298

Each title is subject to availability from Concord Theatricals Corp., depending upon country of performance. Please be aware that *CORSICANA* may not be licensed by Concord Theatricals Corp. in your territory. Professional and amateur producers should contact the nearest Concord Theatricals Corp. office or licensing partner to verify availability.

CAUTION: Professional and amateur producers are hereby warned that *CORSICANA* is subject to a licensing fee. The purchase, renting, lending or use of this book does not constitute a license to perform this title(s), which license must be obtained from Concord Theatricals Corp. prior to any performance. Performance of this title(s) without a license is a violation of federal law and may subject the producer and/or presenter of such performances to civil penalties. Both amateurs and professionals considering a production are strongly advised to apply to the appropriate agent before starting rehearsals, advertising, or booking a theatre. A licensing fee must be paid whether the title(s) is presented for charity or gain and whether or not admission is charged. Professional/Stock licensing fees are quoted upon application to Concord Theatricals Corp.

This work is published by Samuel French, an imprint of Concord Theatricals Corp.

No one shall make any changes in this title(s) for the purpose of production. No part of this book may be reproduced, stored in a retrieval system, scanned, uploaded, or transmitted in any form, by any means, now known or yet to be invented, including mechanical, electronic, digital, photocopying, recording, videotaping, or otherwise, without the prior written permission of the publisher. No one shall share this title(s), or any part of this title(s), through any social media or file hosting websites.

For all inquiries regarding motion picture, television, online/digital and other media rights, please contact Concord Theatricals Corp.

MUSIC AND THIRD-PARTY MATERIALS USE NOTE

Licensees are solely responsible for obtaining formal written permission from copyright owners to use copyrighted music and/or other copyrighted third-party materials (e.g. artworks, logos) in the performance of this play and are strongly cautioned to do so. If no such permission is obtained by the licensee, then the licensee must use only original music and materials that the licensee owns and controls. Licensees are solely responsible and liable for clearances of all third-party copyrighted materials, including without limitation music, and shall indemnify the copyright owners of the play(s) and their licensing agent, Concord Theatricals Corp., against any costs, expenses, losses and liabilities arising from the use of such copyrighted third-party materials by licensees. For music, please contact the appropriate music licensing authority in your territory for the rights to any incidental music.

IMPORTANT BILLING AND CREDIT REQUIREMENTS

If you have obtained performance rights to this title, please refer to your licensing agreement for important billing and credit requirements.

CORSICANA had its world premiere at Playwrights Horizons in New York City on June 22, 2022. It was directed by Sam Gold. The scenic design was by Lael Jellinek and Cate McCrea, the lighting design was by Isabella Byrd, the sound design was by Justin Ellington, and the costume design was by Qween Jean. The composer was Joanna Sternberg. The music director was Ilene Reid, and the vocal and text coach was Gigi Buffington. The production stage manager was Amanda Spooner. The cast was as follows:

GINNY . . . . Jamie Brewer
CHRISTOPHER . . . . Will Dagger
JUSTICE . . . . Deirdre O'Connell
LOT . . . . Harold Surratt

ACKNOWLEDGMENTS

Thank you first and foremost to Sam Gold. This impossible thing happened because of you. Thank you to Amy and Jo. A bottomless thank you to Frances Gold. And thank you to the incredible cast, Will Dagger, Harold Surratt, Didi O'Connell, and Jamie Brewer. This play was you. Thank you Isabella Byrd, Justin Ellington, Lael Jellinek, Cate McCrea, Amanda Spooner, Zach Brecheen, Andie Burns, Joshua Yocom, Ilene Reid, Gigi Buffington, and Qween Jean. Huge thank you to Joanna Sternberg for the gift of your beautiful songs. Thank you Adam Greenfield and Natasha Sinha and Lizzie Stern and Billy McEntee and Blake Zidell and Playwrights Horizons. Thank you Tom Park and David Skinner for your initial support in writing this play. Thank you to Greg Nobile for getting it over the finish line. Thank you to Brian D. Coats, Elizabeth Kenny, Ansa Akyea, K. Todd Freeman, and especially Lauren Potter. Thank you to John MacGregor, Olivier Sultan, Eva Dickerman, Lewis Hyde, Kyle Hobratschk, David Searcy, Nancy Rebal, Wayne Hall, 100W Corsicana, Sam Barickman, Di Glazer, Jacob Robinson, Abigail Friedman, Loddie Allison, Chloé Cooper Jones, Jia Tolentino, Emily Davis, and Ryan Haddad. Thank you to Robert Egan, Mark Seldis, Jose Delgado, Ramon Valdez, Stephen Tyler Howell, and Adam O'Byrne. Thank you to the Ojai Playwrights Conference and Interstate 73. Thank you to Gavin Morrison and Lucia Simek. Special thank you to Joan Arbery and Glenn Arbery and Virginia Arbery. Hi Yi. Love you. Thanks Hilary Duff! Thank you, most especially, to the unstoppable Julia "Joofbox" Arbery, to whom this play is totally & completely dedicated. Pop goes my heart.

CHARACTERS

GINNY – 34, f, white, a woman with Down syndrome, a volunteer, a singer

CHRISTOPHER – 33, m, white, Ginny's half-brother, a film teacher at the community college

JUSTICE – late 60s, f, white, Lot's best friend, Ginny & Christopher's honorary aunt, a writer

LOT – 60s, m, black, an artist, a musician

SETTING

Two spaces in Corsicana, TX:

Lot's house – a barebones space in the middle of nowhere – full of art that we never see.

Ginny's house – one-story, ranch style, doesn't get great light.

TIME

Early summer, 2022.

When you give a gift there is momentum, and the weight shifts from body to body...
The gift moves in a circle...
The gift leaves all boundary and circles into mystery...
– Lewis Hyde, *The Gift*

You just have to say it out loud.
– Julia Arbery

Part One

(Christopher and Ginny's house, which used to be their mom's house: a dusty little Texas ranch-style. **CHRISTOPHER** *is in the den on his phone and* **GINNY** *comes over and looks at him.)*

(He eventually looks up from his phone and touches her nose.)

CHRISTOPHER. Boop.

GINNY. Haha. So.

> *(He notices that she's upset.)*

CHRISTOPHER. Are you okay?

GINNY. I'm not sure.

CHRISTOPHER. What's wrong?

GINNY. I'm not sure. Big hug?

CHRISTOPHER. Yeah.

> *(He gives her a big hug. She cries into his arms. Or maybe she wants to cry but can't.)*

Oh no. Okay. It's okay.

> *(This happens for a while. And then she pulls away.)*

GINNY. I need to do something.

CHRISTOPHER. You need to do something?

GINNY. I need you to help me do something.

CHRISTOPHER. Like what?

GINNY. Something to do.

(She looks at the ground.)

I don't have anything to do.

CHRISTOPHER. Are you bored?

GINNY. No. I'm worried. I can't find my heart.

CHRISTOPHER. Oh. You can't find your heart. Okay –

GINNY. I can't feel anything there.

CHRISTOPHER. Oh no. Okay, so let's get active again. Let's get your job back at the nursing home.

GINNY. No.

CHRISTOPHER. No? What about the choir?

GINNY. No.

CHRISTOPHER. Why not?

GINNY. I don't belong.

CHRISTOPHER. Yes you do. Everyone loves you.

GINNY. Not if I'm not happy.

CHRISTOPHER. They always love you.

GINNY. Not if I'm not like me.

CHRISTOPHER. You don't feel like you?

GINNY. No.

CHRISTOPHER. Oh, man.

GINNY. But that's okay.

CHRISTOPHER. No, it's not. Okay, let's...

(He gets out his phone and starts filming her.)

GINNY. What are you doing?

CHRISTOPHER. Say something to your friends. We'll send it to Tim and Angelo and Justice.

GINNY. What do you want me to say?

CHRISTOPHER. Whatever you want. Something funny.

>   *(Pause.)*

GINNY. *(To the camera.)* Hi, everyone. This is Ginny. I miss you but I need space. I'm not feeling good.

>   *(She covers her face.)*

I hate this.

CHRISTOPHER. *(Still filming.)* Okay just shake it loose. Ginny. HONK! GINNY! What do you wanna say to your BOYS!

>   *(She doesn't show her face. He keeps trying. He tries to get the camera in her face to make her laugh, and she pushes it away. He stops filming.)*

Sorry.

GINNY. It's okay.

CHRISTOPHER. I'm sorry, Ginny.

GINNY. It's not a big deal.

CHRISTOPHER. No, it is. Have I been –

GINNY. Have you been what?

CHRISTOPHER. Just kind of. Asleep.

GINNY. No you're awake.

CHRISTOPHER. No I'm so...

GINNY. I'm just not in the mood.

CHRISTOPHER. Yeah.

GINNY. Because I'm lazy.

CHRISTOPHER. No you're not. I am.

GINNY. Yeah you are.

CHRISTOPHER. You think I'm lazy?

GINNY. Just a little bit.

CHRISTOPHER. Yeah we're just... Okay. We need to – we're just, like, little kids. We don't know what to do. Like we're waiting for her to come in and just be like, *let's eat, let's go to church, let's*... but we're just little kids.

GINNY. No, we're adults.

CHRISTOPHER. You're right.

GINNY. I'm thirty-four years old and you're thirty-three years old.

CHRISTOPHER. You're right.

GINNY. So we have to be adults.

CHRISTOPHER. Okay.

GINNY. So you have to figure that out.

CHRISTOPHER. Okay I get it.

GINNY. And shave your face.

CHRISTOPHER. What? No.

GINNY. Are you sure?

CHRISTOPHER. You don't like the mustache?

GINNY. No. But I'm open-minded, actually. So be yourself.

CHRISTOPHER. Okay...

GINNY. I can help you to be yourself. I need you to help me to be myself. And that's hard for me to say, because I don't like asking for help.

CHRISTOPHER. Okay. I understand. And I'm sorry for being lazy and scared.

GINNY. That's fine.

CHRISTOPHER. Okay. I'm gonna – okay.

> *(Now:)*

> *(**JUSTICE** is unloading groceries in their kitchen. **CHRISTOPHER** enters in his sleep clothes.)*

JUSTICE. Oh, sorry!

CHRISTOPHER. What are you –

JUSTICE. Nothing to see here.

CHRISTOPHER. You didn't have to do that.

JUSTICE. Just a few things. I was already there.

CHRISTOPHER. Oh man thanks, Justice. Thanks. Yeah sorry – I think I took on too many classes.

> *(He holds up some Sprite.*)*

Oh thanks. Oh is this for Ginny?

JUSTICE. She asked for it directly.

CHRISTOPHER. I'm trying to get her off soda. Is that dumb?

JUSTICE. No that's probably very not dumb. Should I take it back?

CHRISTOPHER. Yeah maybe. Is that okay?

JUSTICE. Sure, I'll give it to the church. Or I like Sprite.

CHRISTOPHER. I just think it's not good for her. I don't know. Whatever I don't know.

---

* A license to produce *CORSICANA* does not include a license to publicly display any branded logos or trademarked images. Licensees must acquire rights for any logos and/or images or create their own.

JUSTICE. Did you talk to her about it?

CHRISTOPHER. I tried. No, I don't know. I just thought I'd wean her off it slowly. Like be a better influence. It's dumb it's manipulative. I just want her to feel better.

JUSTICE. And you?

CHRISTOPHER. Me? No, I eat terribly, I'm a huge hypocrite.

JUSTICE. No, how are *you* feeling?

CHRISTOPHER. Oh. I mean who can say.

JUSTICE. Uh-huh.

CHRISTOPHER. What about you?

JUSTICE. Heavy. Slow to joy. Missing your mom. More than I know what to do with.

CHRISTOPHER. Yeah. It's.

JUSTICE. Yeah. Don't know where to put it all.

CHRISTOPHER. Yeah, exactly. It's.

> *(Pause.)*

Sorry. It's hard for me to, uh –

JUSTICE. Don't be sorry.

CHRISTOPHER. Ginny said I'm lazy.

JUSTICE. You're not lazy.

CHRISTOPHER. I think I am. I know I am. HEB is literally on the way home from work, it's right there, I could just go in and get groceries and I don't. I don't make things better. And what am I, the king of dust?

JUSTICE. Ha! Well there's a writer I love who calls dust "matter in the wrong place." And laziness "temperament not aligning with environment." Shut up, Justice. I thought we had a plan, Christopher. I thought you liked that idea of going to see Lot.

CHRISTOPHER. Yeah I did like that idea. I'm just nervous. But let's do it.

JUSTICE. No I'm not coming with you.

CHRISTOPHER. Really?

JUSTICE. No he won't talk to you if I'm there. He's too used to me. He'll answer all your questions right to my face.

CHRISTOPHER. Is he mean?

JUSTICE. Nahhh.

CHRISTOPHER. Okay. Okay I'll go. I'm just nervous. I mean it feels weird to just show up and – but it's the best idea we've got and I'm gonna go I'm just nervous.

JUSTICE. No, don't be nervous. Look, you drive that long road and it feels like nothing at first. And then suddenly it's just something. And it's great. He's great. Something's shifted in him lately. He's letting himself be seen. And letting me spend whole days with him, and it's been… it's really been – well. Who knows. You're gonna love him, Christopher. I have a good feeling about it.

CHRISTOPHER. That's good.

JUSTICE. Just see how it feels.

CHRISTOPHER. Okay.

JUSTICE. I have a good feeling about it.

CHRISTOPHER. Do you?

JUSTICE. Sort of a dream.

CHRISTOPHER. Yeah. What?

JUSTICE. Like a dream. Like I dreamt it. Like I dreamt it already happened and it went great. Don't know if I really did dream it, all I can remember for sure from my dreams lately is circles, circles of bodies, standing, bodies of the dead standing in circles. But not in a bad way. And this feels part of that. So I feel good. Like I know what's gonna happen already, even though I don't know, and it's good, and I'm just impatient to get to that goodness. And it's *very* selfish. Like good things come out of it for me. I feel implicated. But first you gotta go do your thing. Then I'll know what my thing is. But no rush, I can wait. And I might be wrong about all this. I'm just meddlesome. I'm just guessing.

> *(Now:)*

> (**CHRISTOPHER** *steps into Lot's small house, which is full of art and some trash that will soon be art. But we don't see any of it.)*

CHRISTOPHER. Hello...?

LOT. *(Offstage.)* What. Dangit. Who – uh – oh – I'm not wearing pants – who is that –

CHRISTOPHER. It's uh –

LOT. *(Offstage.)* I'm not wearing pants –

CHRISTOPHER. Sorry!

LOT. *(Offstage.)* Who uh – one moment.

> (**LOT** *emerges from his secret workspace. He's wearing pants.)*

Who's that?

CHRISTOPHER. Hi, sorry. I would have called but –

LOT. Yeah no telephone –

CHRISTOPHER. Yeah of course, so I'm sorry for – So – so –

LOT. You saw that article? Is that all happening now?

CHRISTOPHER. Oh, no I – do you remember – no, Justice introduced us, we met in the street fair, last month. We talked about uh, I was the one you played that song for –

LOT. Oh.

CHRISTOPHER. Do you remember? That beautiful song?

LOT. I played it?

CHRISTOPHER. Yeah by the – by Justice's book sale... Justice is a friend of my family's.

LOT. Justice is a friend of everyone's family.

CHRISTOPHER. That's true. But she's like really sort of a part of mine.

LOT. Well me too. So?

CHRISTOPHER. Oh but anyway –

LOT. Which song?

CHRISTOPHER. Oh, it was, it was beautiful. I think it was called "Weird."

LOT. Yeah, oh yeah, yeah, "Weird." I remember you. I played you "Weird."

CHRISTOPHER. Yeah, I loved it. I'm sorry for just showing up, I just didn't know –

LOT. It's fine.

CHRISTOPHER. Oh good yeah Justice said to just show up, so –

LOT. Yeah that's fine – the gate's open at the front, that means you're welcome. I keep it open now. Visitors welcome.

CHRISTOPHER. Great, good –

LOT. Anyway I was ready. There's been a question in the air lately.

CHRISTOPHER. Oh yeah?

LOT. Yeah so I didn't know what to expect with a question in the air – so I've been working hard and just working hard and harder – getting weird and working hard – so I didn't know what to expect – when there's a question like that in the air.

CHRISTOPHER. What – uh – sorry what question?

LOT. About whether people'd be showing up. I was grieving but it was closing me up. Now I want the grieving to open me up. And I opened my heart up and then the article happened.

CHRISTOPHER. Oh I'm sorry to hear you've been grieving. I am too.

LOT. That's okay.

CHRISTOPHER. Yeah. Well – yeah Justice showed me that article in *Oxford American* and it was really so good. Like so cool. So so cool. It really made me proud to be from Corsicana. And the whole layout, the spread, the art looked so good, it was so cool and so fancy. And yeah just congratulations and yeah just like what's it like to be so fancy?

LOT. Is it so absurd that The Fancy and I could commingle?

CHRISTOPHER. Oh not at all, sorry if I... oh wait I recognize some of these guys! This is the same art here that was in the – it's right here!

LOT. Some of it. The rest she took away in a box.

CHRISTOPHER. Oh cool, to show it? That's awesome.

LOT. You're enthusiastic.

CHRISTOPHER. I am?

LOT. The word "enthusiasm" means "possessed by God."

CHRISTOPHER. Oh, cool. How'd this writer find you?

LOT. It's all Justice's fault. Some friend of Justice, some friend from Dallas who saw my things. She came down, poked around, saw what I'd – yeah. And I guess she – yeah. She had a lot of ideas about what it all meant. And she wrote down the ideas and came back down and we went through it together. With a pen. And some of it felt okay to me.

CHRISTOPHER. Really special.

LOT. Not *special.*

CHRISTOPHER. What?

LOT. Not *special.*

It's not *special.*

It just *is.*

Not *special* it just *is.*

CHRISTOPHER. Right. Sorry.

LOT. Well she has whole books full of that kind of thinking. I fit into some vision she had of the world and what's beautiful in it.

CHRISTOPHER. Yeah I mean I wish I fit into someone's uh –

LOT. Why are you here?

CHRISTOPHER. Okay right uh – my name is Christopher and I was wondering if you'd want to um – if you were in the position to – like if you were looking for – I was wondering if I could give you a little work?

LOT. Your work?

CHRISTOPHER. What?

LOT. Work you made? You want to give it to me?

CHRISTOPHER. Oh – no – what I meant was I was wondering if I could, like, *employ* you. Like a part-time gig thing – just like if you're not too busy.

LOT. What kinda work?

CHRISTOPHER. Well – yeah! I know you're getting all famous for your sculptures but it's, uh, it's actually about your music. You're such a multi-hyphenate, it's intimidating.

LOT. I'm a what?

CHRISTOPHER. Just – I thought your song was really beautiful, obviously – and I wonder if you'd want to collaborate with my sister? Musically? Or just spend some time?

LOT. Your sister? Spend some time –

CHRISTOPHER. Sure, yeah, just spend some time, and maybe make things together – or get her in the making mood – get her making… I could pay you, to help her get creative?

LOT. Get creative?

CHRISTOPHER. She loves music – she really loves music.

LOT. Okay.

CHRISTOPHER. And I'm sure you two have wildly different taste, but – maybe you could help her make some music.

LOT. Like lessons?

CHRISTOPHER. If you want!

LOT. Or what?

CHRISTOPHER. Lessons – or just, just hanging out – while I'm at work? Or – making a song together.

LOT. Is it hanging out or is it making something?

CHRISTOPHER. I think making a song?

LOT. Just one song?

CHRISTOPHER. Yeah I mean I think one song would feel momentous. Like for her to say, "look I made this." She's a natural performer. And then maybe I could make a music video for the song. I make – I mean I work at the community college – I teach film.

LOT. At Navarro?

CHRISTOPHER. Yeah, I used to teach in Dallas, actually – well, Denton. I was making more stuff there. We had a production company. My friend and I. "Elbow Productions." It's an inside joke.

LOT. Okay.

CHRISTOPHER. I met him at UNT. Yeah he might come down and we might make something. Like a horror. This town would be great for a horror. But it's hard. There's *some* film stuff happening here – well not Corsicana but Dallas – greater Dallas – the metroplex – but you know, not like LA. Plus I fell out with some of those guys. Even before I had to move down here.

LOT. Why are you telling me the novel of you?

CHRISTOPHER. Oh sorry! Different art scenes I guess. I mean yeah – Ginny just needs something to do. Yeah our mom passed away last Christmas and she – yeah they were like *this*. And now she doesn't have her buddy. And neither of our dads are in the picture. And she's – she's grieving, she's...uh. I've never seen her like this and I want to get her brain, uh – or just – get her social – give her some structure.

LOT. Sounds like babysitting.

CHRISTOPHER. It's not – no – that's not what this is. It's *artistic*.

LOT. Is this something she wants to do?

CHRISTOPHER. I think so, I think she'd enjoy it.

LOT. How old is she?

CHRISTOPHER. She's thirty-four.

LOT. *(After a beat.)* Why do you want me to babysit your grown-ass sister?

CHRISTOPHER. No! Oh – sorry. I didn't explain. She has Down syndrome. It's not babysitting, and please, don't call it that around her. But she has – yeah, she has Down syndrome.

(**LOT** *nods. Spits.*)

LOT. "Special needs."

CHRISTOPHER. Right, yeah.

LOT. Yeah I know "special needs." Why'd you come here? I know the place in the high school. The hallway in the high school. You know I'm not one of them, right?

CHRISTOPHER. What?

LOT. I'm not special needs.

CHRISTOPHER. Oh – I didn't think you were. I assumed the opposite.

LOT. What's the opposite? I was only a couple years in that hallway. And they knew I didn't belong. Got a graduate degree in my forties. So don't worry about me.

CHRISTOPHER. Oh, cool. In what?

LOT. Experimental mathematics. I proved the existence of God.

CHRISTOPHER. Are you serious? Can I see?

LOT. I threw it away. Art's a better delivery system. It's Down syndrome?

CHRISTOPHER. Yeah.

LOT. And it's about making a song that's hers.

CHRISTOPHER. A song that's hers. Yeah. Like how cool would that be.

LOT. I never did anything like this. This isn't what I was expecting at all.

CHRISTOPHER. Yeah –

LOT. Don't think I'd be good.

CHRISTOPHER. I bet you would be.

LOT. You don't know.

CHRISTOPHER. That's true – but Justice said that you're one of the best people ever, pretty much, so –

LOT. Justice is biased.

CHRISTOPHER. Maybe so.

LOT. Justice is just my friend, that's what.

CHRISTOPHER. Well she spoke very highly of you.

LOT. Justice and I, we agreed, we believe in gifts, not capital. It's a prison. To consume, to consume. And then evacuate. To toss out. It's sinful. It's man-made. It's all a man-made evil.

CHRISTOPHER. Oh okay – yeah…

LOT. So think of a gift to give me in return. One day down the line. That's the rubric.

CHRISTOPHER. Oh really? Okay I will. I absolutely will. Does this mean you're –

LOT. Making one song with one person. Fine. Good for me if it's good for her. What's her name?

CHRISTOPHER. Her name is Ginny.

LOT. How often you thinking for Ginny?

CHRISTOPHER. Well I teach four days a week – but it could be – we could try it out slower. Yeah, something slower, to respect your time. Mondays only or something?

LOT. Mondays I could do. Let's start with Mondays or some shit.

Hell – now I have to start knowing what day is Monday.

Hell – now I have to get a calendar or something.

And keep track of what day is Monday – hell.

    (Now:)

*(**CHRISTOPHER** standing in the threshold, looking at **GINNY**.)*

CHRISTOPHER. Ginny, I made an appointment for you on Monday. With a musician. His name is Lot. He's Justice's friend. He's gonna make a song with you.

GINNY. A song?

CHRISTOPHER. Yeah. Doesn't that sound fun?

GINNY. Not really.

CHRISTOPHER. Okay. Well can you just go? He's excited to meet you. The song can be about everything you're feeling right now. I think it's good – you know? It's good, I think, to try to make something out of – I don't know. Right?

GINNY. I get it. I'll go.

CHRISTOPHER. Okay. Really? Okay cool. Thank you.

*(**CHRISTOPHER** turns to leave.)*

GINNY. But I did have a nightmare that you ran away.

CHRISTOPHER. What?

GINNY. Mom always loved to take me on girl dates and say that men run away. That's what they do.

CHRISTOPHER. But I'm not gonna – Ginny, I'm right here.

(Now:)

*(**CHRISTOPHER**'s gone. **JUSTICE** is there, eating Sonic.* **GINNY**'s singing a pop country song by a band like The Chicks to herself.**)*

---

* A license to produce *CORSICANA* does not include a license to publicly display any branded logos or trademarked images. Licensees must acquire rights for any logos and/or images or create their own.

** A license to produce *CORSICANA* does not include a performance license for any third-party or copyrighted music. Licensees should create an original composition or use music in the public domain. For further information, please see the Music and Third-Party Materials Use Note on page iii.

(The CD starts skipping. A word in the song repeats over and over.)

GINNY. OH COME ON. I HATE THIS. I HATE MYSELF.

JUSTICE. No you don't!

GINNY. Is that Justice?

JUSTICE. Yes!

*(**GINNY** finds **JUSTICE**.)*

GINNY. Why are you here?

JUSTICE. I'm babysitting you!

GINNY. I'M AN ADULT.

*(**GINNY** storms off.)*

I NEED SOME SPACE.

JUSTICE. YOU'RE RIGHT! I APOLOGIZE.

(To herself:) Come on, Justice.

(Now:)

*(**JUSTICE** is in Lot's space. He's mixing glue.)*

I tell you what happened with the dead man? I was getting ready for a bash, some donor for the library was throwing some kinda bash?

LOT. Is this a dream?

JUSTICE. No – not a dream.

LOT. Real life?

JUSTICE. I don't know – maybe. I guess so.

LOT. You're weird.

JUSTICE. Whatever. So I was looking in the mirror like *how much am I gonna wanna dance tonight, how much am I gonna wanna be moving around?* And then back

behind me in the mirror suddenly it's a man holding
out a dress for me. Yeah. And what's funny is that
at first I'm like – *hell that's my only dress, nah, pick
something else, I haven't worn that since my forties, I
don't wear a dress unless forced* – I think maybe even I
say that out loud before I realize, like, okay, um *what!*
There's a man in my room! And then I turn around and
he's not there of course.

LOT. Is this real?

JUSTICE. Let me finish.

LOT. You're weird.

JUSTICE. But what's interesting is in that moment upon
realizing his presence, I felt like I knew exactly who
he was in my life. He was someone very specific to me,
someone I was used to having around. And now for the
life of me I can't remember who he was, to me, in that
moment – but the *feeling*, the comfort of being with
him, felt like it had a full *lifetime* of evidence behind it.

LOT. Who was it?

JUSTICE. Shut up!

LOT. I just think you're weird. I just don't know why you're
not telling me if this is real or not.

JUSTICE. It's real. Okay? It's real – everything's real. It's all
real to me. You're the one who showed me how to pay
closer attention to these things. So shut up.

So. It wasn't the *seeing* of him that was scary, it was
the *forgetting* of how I knew him... I was much more
scared of my brain afterwards, than my brain during.
You know?

LOT. No.

JUSTICE. And then I saw him again. *Been* seeing him
around – in church, at the library, in front of my
headlights at night – and every time it's like a prayer
when you really get inside it – a sort of cave you get

into, or a bubble floating in space, for a few minutes you get inside a bubble, which is its own world unto itself, nothing getting in or out, except *you* get in, and *you* get out – but you can't remember what it was like inside there. You know?

LOT. ...yeah. *That* I know.

JUSTICE. I know. *That* you know. It's a funny feeling. You know that you went *in* there, and you know that you feel different *now*, but you don't know how you felt *then*.

That's what's started happening with this dead man. Makes it non-catastrophic, somehow. He's scary as hell, but he doesn't have power. I can fear him and want him at the same time. I can love how he makes me feel, and not *know* how he makes me feel, all at the same time. I just look forward to seeing him because I know I'm gonna feel *some* type of way. And then when he's gone I can't remember how it was that I felt. Only that I'm breathing slower and my spine is numb.

LOT. Could be a vitamin deficiency. Maybe you just need to eat more fish.

JUSTICE. Shut up. I saw him out on my lawn though yesterday which is why it's forefront in my mind. He was interrogating the air. I don't know how else to put it – he had the air around us pinned down and he was interrogating it. Which I think made me feel interrogated as well. Something was wanted from me, in a way it hadn't been before. I was pulled to the earth fast. Knees first. Skinned my knees.

> *(She pulls up her pants and examines her skinned knees. **LOT** looks at them.)*

LOT. You okay?

JUSTICE. I'm okay, of course.

LOT. You can't remember how you know him?

JUSTICE. Who said I know him?

LOT. I thought you did.

JUSTICE. No I don't know that for sure. Or whether it's *me* who's doing the knowing. Might be that someone else takes over, in those moments, and *they're* the one who knows him. I dunno.

LOT. But you feel okay with him.

JUSTICE. So far. Learning as I go.

LOT. I just don't want him to switch all the sudden and get angry.

JUSTICE. I don't see that happening.

LOT. Well.

JUSTICE. Well, we'll see.

LOT. We will.

(**LOT** *goes back into his secret workspace.*)

I'm gonna start a new job soon I guess.

JUSTICE. What's that?

LOT. *(Offstage.)* I think you might be responsible.

JUSTICE. How so?

LOT. *(Offstage.)* You told some guy that I was trustworthy.

JUSTICE. I did?

LOT. *(Offstage.)* Some guy from Navarro, he's got a special sister.

JUSTICE. Oh yeah, that guy, yeah he was asking after you.

(**LOT** *comes back out.*)

LOT. You don't have to lie.

JUSTICE. About what?

LOT. I know he's like family to you, not just some guy.

JUSTICE. Yeah okay whatever. I just didn't want you to think I was pulling strings.

LOT. Well are you?

JUSTICE. No, Christopher was asking about you!

LOT. Okay. You know I kinda struggle sometimes.

JUSTICE. I know.

LOT. I don't know what I can teach this girl.

JUSTICE. Just see where it takes you.

LOT. Okay.

JUSTICE. Big year. Getting your art out there. Meeting new people. Collaborating. You given any more thought to the idea of a little gallery showing?

LOT. Don't wanna think about that right now.

JUSTICE. Okay. Just let me know when you're ready and I'll call Gail for you.

LOT. Okay. Gotta ask though.

JUSTICE. Okay.

LOT. About this girl.

JUSTICE. Ginny, okay, yeah.

LOT. Why's he asking me to, uh – with this Down syndrome... does he think *I'm* –

JUSTICE. Does he think you're what?

LOT. I dunno. Sometimes I just can't tell my place in things.

JUSTICE. Your place in things is wherever you want it to be, just like anyone.

LOT. Okay. Thank you for the sermonizing.

JUSTICE. What sermonizing?

LOT. Forget it.

JUSTICE. Okay well I think I'm a haunted troll and I think you're brilliant and I think we're peas in a pod. You and I. That's all.

LOT. I've never been peas in a pod with anyone.

JUSTICE. Well I think you are with me.

LOT. I don't know about that.

JUSTICE. Forget I said it.

LOT. I will.

JUSTICE. Is she coming here?

LOT. Well I'm not going *there*.

JUSTICE. Hell you gotta clean this place up then.

LOT. What? No.

>   *(Now:)*

>   *(**GINNY** is in Lot's house. They stare at each other a while before they speak.)*

So what kinda things you like.

GINNY. What?

LOT. What kinda – what kinda things you like?

GINNY. Oh, I don't know.

LOT. Oh yeah?

>   *(Pause.)*

GINNY. I like listening to music.

LOT. Is that all you like?

GINNY. No.

LOT. Okay. What else you like?

GINNY. Lots of stuff.

LOT. Mhm.

>   *(Pause.)*

One thing I like is I like making things with my hands.

GINNY. Right. What things?

LOT. I make things, I don't know. I just make them.

GINNY. Yeah. I like your shirt.

LOT. What?

GINNY. I like your shirt.

LOT. I guess it's an okay shirt...

GINNY. Yeah.

LOT. I didn't make it.

>   *(**GINNY** laughs nervously. **LOT** gets very uncomfortable. **GINNY** gets out her iPad and starts watching something.*)*

What are you doing?

GINNY. Watching Disney Channel.

LOT. Oh. How?

GINNY. This is my iPad from my mom.

LOT. But I don't have internet.

GINNY. We downloaded it to watch in the car.

LOT. Oh.

>   *(**GINNY** watches the show. Silence. **LOT** goes into his secret workspace and starts working on a sculpture. **GINNY** gets bored and sad.)*

GINNY. When is my brother coming?

---

* A license to produce *CORSICANA* does not include a performance license for any third-party or copyrighted recordings. Licensees should create their own.

LOT. I don't know. Later. This was dumb.

GINNY. I don't like that word.

LOT. Okay.

GINNY. And I don't actually know you.

LOT. That's because we've never met.

> *(Now:)*

> *(***CHRISTOPHER***'s picking **GINNY** up. She's in the bathroom.)*

I don't want to keep doing this.

CHRISTOPHER. Oh. No? Why not?

LOT. Just don't.

CHRISTOPHER. Oh, okay…that's…hm. Okay. Shoot. Are you sure?

LOT. She just sat there and watched something called *Jessie* for three hours. I think I'm just her babysitter. And if I'm doing that I should get paid capital just for being, uh – useless. Money is only good for useless people.

CHRISTOPHER. You're not useless. You're not a babysitter. And I could absolutely pay you if… look I'm sorry it didn't go well but I think you just have to get into a groove, right? She won't have her iPad next time.

LOT. Well I don't think she has much interest.

CHRISTOPHER. In what?

LOT. Anything.

CHRISTOPHER. She has a lot of interest. In a lot of things. She hasn't been herself. It's –

LOT. Nah I get the feeling that she doesn't like me.

CHRISTOPHER. Is that the issue?

LOT. Yeah.

CHRISTOPHER. Well that's easy. Ginny!

> *(The toilet flushes.* **GINNY** *comes out.)*

GINNY. Okay, that bathroom has some monsters in it.

LOT. Those are sculptures.

GINNY. Oh that's okay.

CHRISTOPHER. Ginny do you like Lot?

GINNY. Who?

CHRISTOPHER. Lot – right here, asshole.

GINNY. *(After a beat.)* Hm…

LOT. See? She doesn't like me.

CHRISTOPHER. Yes she *does.*

GINNY. I do.

CHRISTOPHER. She does.

GINNY. Yeah. Kind of a lot. And I want to make a song. We have to get to work and not be shy.

LOT. I'm not shy I just miss my Mondays, dangit. Fine. This is what you get. This what you get when you say okay.

> *(Now:)*

> *(The next Monday.* **GINNY** *has paper and pencils in front of her. She starts tapping one of the pencils.)*

One thing I sometimes want to write about is how I lost my best friend.

GINNY. Oh wow.

LOT. Yeah. Her name was Mary Ellen. She lived over there. I miss her. She was my mother. She was a miracle and a maniac.

GINNY. A what?

LOT. A miracle and a maniac.

GINNY. That's awesome.

LOT. Yeah, just my best friend. She died twelve years ago.

GINNY. Oh I can't believe that. Do you want a hug?

LOT. No thanks. Can't believe he got her.

GINNY. Oh, right.

LOT. Don't you wanna know who got her?

GINNY. Who?

LOT. Well in the 1880s a one-legged man showed up in town and tightrope-walked across Main Street and fell to his death. He's buried in the cemetery not too far from my mother. Nobody knew his name, so all it says on the stone is: ROPE WALKER. He came to town and hung the rope. He told the town to watch him walk it. Then he fell. But what no one knows is: he didn't fall, he was pushed.

GINNY. Are you kidding? By who?

LOT. Dinosaur. Anyone who lives here long enough knows that there are dinosaur ghosts all around us. And they been here for a long time but they get wiser the longer they stay. Sad ghosts of dinosaurs. They can't die and they just get wiser so they just get sadder. There used to be a Ku Klux Klan group that met right in the center of town. And one time they were having a ritual and nearly burned the town down because their building set on fire. They were doing their hateful things and suddenly they all felt enormous wings flapping around them. Their candles fell and were burning their garments and banners and things. They all swore they were being attacked by what felt like a giant bat. And they had gashes on their skin to prove it. But it wasn't a bat, it was a pterodactyl. So now you know.

(Pause.)

GINNY. Your mom got eaten by a dinosaur?

LOT. Kinda. Felt like it.

GINNY. That's kinda scary.

LOT. Wanna sing about it?

GINNY. No.

LOT. Yeah, right, that was my thing. What about one of your things? Wanna sing about having Down syndrome?

GINNY. Huh? No.

LOT. Yeah.

GINNY. Or maybe so.

LOT. Okay.

GINNY. I can talk, not sing.

LOT. Okay, talk.

GINNY. Okay. So just talking? Fine. About what? Fine.

I'm not the only one who has Down syndrome. I've been this way my entire life.

It's hard for some people to understand, they don't know how to react. But it means I'm special and I have some problems – shaking problems, and a good imagination, like I can't control my body at night, and sometimes I cry and cough. And I'm healthy.

The best thing about being a woman with Down syndrome is being smart, and doing lots of special things for people, and helping old people, helping others.

I'm happy God made me how I am because I have blue eyes. And I am sensitive.

My heart is like this dream-wish about things. The best thing about my heart is that I can talk to anybody.

LOT. I think that can be a song.

GINNY. Like what?

LOT. Like:

[MUSIC #1 – I'M NOT THE ONLY ONE]

(Singing:)

I'M NOT THE ONLY ONE WHO HAS DOWN SYNDROME
NO, I'M NOT THE ONLY ONE WHO HAS DOWN SYNDROME –

GINNY. Okay – no.

LOT. No?

GINNY. No. No.

LOT. Okay.

GINNY. Your voice is weird.

LOT. Oh.

GINNY. I like it.

LOT. Thanks.

GINNY. I don't know. I don't want to sing about Down syndrome. Maybe my half-brother. Or my friends. Maybe my mom.

LOT. You wanna write about your mom?

GINNY. Actually, no.

LOT. Or your brother?

GINNY. Okay!

LOT. Okay.

GINNY. Christopher's a good half-brother, um... I don't like when he's lazy and doesn't know how to be an adult. I like when he takes me to see the movies and I wish he didn't get so upset about his students. But he has dreams about true love and I know we'll get there together.

LOT. Yeah.

GINNY. Yeah.

LOT. You wanna just sing?

You wanna just sing some of your thoughts about Christopher?

Like I'll show you. Like I'll do it about my friend Justice. Like:

(He starts singing. It's impromptu and weird but awesome.)

[MUSIC #2 – JUSTICE IS A FRIEND]

JUSTICE IS A FRIEND TO ME
JUSTICE MADE A HOME FOR ME
JUSTICE IS A FRIEND

I NEEDED SOMEWHERE TO SLEEP
NEEDED SOMEWHERE TO MAKE A MESS
NEEDED SOME PLACE TO CALL MY OWN

WEIRD WITHOUT MY FAMILY
WEIRD WITH MY MAMA DEAD
MY SISTER GONE TO LITTLE ROCK
WAS GETTING WEIRD THAT DAY
WEIRD BEFORE THE PEOPLE KNEW
JUST WHO I AM OR WHAT I DO
NO ONE KNEW A THING 'BOUT ME
MY SISTER GONE MY FAMILY DEAD

JUSTICE FOUND ME A GOOD LOT
AND JUSTICE SAID THIS IS LOT'S LOT
JUSTICE FOUND ME A GOOD PRICE

SHE WENT IN AND RAISED THE FRAME
A COUPLE BOYS FROM TOWN THEY CAME
AND LIFTED THE HOUSE UP FOR ME

THE SUN WAS HOT WE DRANK A LOT
OZARKA, OZARKA, WATER JUG,
DISTILLED OZARKA

LOT.

> JUSTICE! OH JUSTICE!
> SHE GAVE THE KEY FOR THE GATE
> SHOULD I EVER NEED TO LOCK UP
> OR FEEL LIKE KEEPING PEOPLE OUT

> *(He stops singing.)*

GINNY. Well that was okay I guess!

LOT. Think you can do something like that?

> Just sing your thoughts. Just sing your thoughts as they come to you.

GINNY. I can't.

LOT. I think you can.

GINNY. I don't know.

> *(She starts singing "Come Clean" by Hilary Duff.)*

> LET'S GO BACK, BACK TO THE BEGINNING,
> BACK TO WHEN THE EARTH, THE SUN, THE STARS
> ALL ALIGNED
> 'CAUSE PERFECT DIDN'T FEEL SO PERFECT
> AND TRYING TO FIT A SQUARE INTO A CIRCLE WAS NO LIFE
> I DEFY...
> LET THE RAIN FALL DOWN AND WAKE MY DREAMS
> LET IT WASH AWAY MY SANITY
> 'CAUSE I WANNA FEEL THE THUNDER I WANNA SCREAM
> LET THE RAIN FALL DOWN, I'M COMING CLEAN
> I'M COMING CLEAN

LOT. That was incredible.

GINNY. That was Hilary Duff.

LOT. Who?

GINNY. Hilary Duff.

LOT. Who's that?

GINNY. Lizzie McGuire.

LOT. You didn't write that?

GINNY. No.

LOT. Dang.

> *(Now:)*

> *(The next day. **JUSTICE** in Lot's house. Holding a bag.)*

JUSTICE. Want a burrito? I have an extra.

LOT. *(Taking it.)* Okay, maybe.

JUSTICE. Eat it, art monk. Do you have that Kropotkin book I gave you?

LOT. What book?

JUSTICE. Peter Kropotkin. *The Conquest of Bread*. Pyotr. Pyotr Kropot–

LOT. Oh that. I used that. Tore out the pages and glued them on my thing.

JUSTICE. What?

LOT. I apologize.

JUSTICE. Lot, that was from the library.

LOT. I apologize.

JUSTICE. I'm the head librarian!

LOT. I apologize.

JUSTICE. Whatever. Let me see what it became.

LOT. No it's not ready! You're not allowed to look back there.

JUSTICE. Whatever. Did you read it at least?

LOT. As I was tearing and gluing it on.

JUSTICE. Did you like it?

LOT. Socialism. Scarcity. Sharing. Bread. Sure. You trying to get me to believe in community?

JUSTICE. No. I have no agenda.

LOT. Uh-huh.

JUSTICE. What do you have against community?

LOT. I don't have to have all the same opinions as you.

JUSTICE. Didn't say you did! How's it going with Ginny?

LOT. I don't know. Fine.

JUSTICE. You enjoying it?

LOT. Guess so.

JUSTICE. Good. Y'all writing a song?

LOT. How do I know? It's gonna take years. It's gonna take twelve thousand years. You're giving me anxiety. Light's dying. I have things to do.

JUSTICE. Alright alright. Just eat the burrito. Don't make it art, art monk. Eat the burrito, cowboy. Eat it.

> *(Now:)*

> *(**LOT** is recording a song on a tape recorder. He's playing a raw melody on a little keyboard.)*

[MUSIC #3 – A GREAT WALL OF TRASH]

LOT. *(Singing.)*
A GREAT WALL OF TRASH APPEARED 'ROUND THE TOWN
I COULDN'T GET PAST THAT BIG SMELLY MOUND
I WAS THINKIN' HOW STRANGE
THIS GREAT WALL OF TRASH
SO I CUT THE WALL DOWN
WITH MY LITTLE EYELASH

IT TOOK A LONG TIME
IT TOOK A LONG TIME
IT TOOK A LONG TIME
IT TOOK A LONG TIME

SO I PACKED IT ALL UP
AND I BROUGHT THE TRASH HOME
TRASH OLDER THAN ME
TRASH OLD AS THE SEA

WEIRDOS DON'T ASK FOR HELP
NO ONE KNEW IT WAS ME
BUT I SHOULDN'T COMPLAIN
NOW THE PEOPLE ARE FREE

> *(Now:)*

> *(**GINNY** and **LOT** are in Lot's house. New session.)*

Did you listen to that tape I gave you?

GINNY. What tape?

LOT. I gave you a tape. I sent you home with a tape. It has three songs on it.

GINNY. Oh, I'm not sure.

LOT. You didn't listen to them?

GINNY. No.

LOT. Dangit! I made those songs for you. I wrote three songs for you.

GINNY. Oh, I know.

LOT. And you didn't listen to them?

GINNY. Not yet. I will.

LOT. This is proof about how talking to people is stupid.

GINNY. Please don't say "stupid."

LOT. Why not?

GINNY. I don't like it, please.

LOT. Okay. Do you think my songs are weird? Maybe you think the songs are weird.

GINNY. A little.

LOT. Okay.

GINNY. Yeah.

LOT. You don't like the way I make music.

GINNY. Not really.

LOT. Okay.

GINNY. Yeah.

LOT. I was never trained. So maybe that's why.

GINNY. I like music with more music. And stuff like that.

LOT. Music with more music?

GINNY. I like Celine Dion, NSYNC, Selena Gomez – stuff like that.

LOT. Okay.

GINNY. Hilary Duff, Shawn Mendes, Whitney Houston – stuff like that.

LOT. Right. Who are these people? Whitney Houston I know.

GINNY. Yeah, Whitney Houston.

LOT. Whitney Houston I know. My sister loved her.

GINNY. Right.

LOT. But who's Shawn Mendes?

GINNY. He sings like Prince Legolas.

LOT. Who's that?

GINNY. My husband.

LOT. What?

GINNY. Orlando Bloom. I like when music makes me think about God and dance for my mom. And I don't twerk or stuff like that. My friend Angelo twerks like crazy. And stuff like that.

LOT. I get it. You like pop.

GINNY. There ya go.

LOT. Well I'm not the right person to be teaching anyone pop.

GINNY. But I like country.

LOT. You like country?

GINNY. Yes. Shania Twain, and Dixie Chicks, and Carrie Underwood.

LOT. Oh I don't know them.

GINNY. Who's your favorite singer?

LOT. My favorite singer? Yeah. What's his name?

GINNY. I don't know.

LOT. Well, whatever. I liked my grandfather's voice. Last night I had a dream that I wasn't wearing any shoes, and I was in a room with my grandfather.

And other old men.

And other old men, in a circle.

And they started singing.

Low. Low singing. For a long time.

A low sort of dead singing. For a long time.

I think my favorite music is music like that.

GINNY. Well, that's cool.

LOT. Not really. I don't know anyone's names. I like the song about waiting round to die.

GINNY. Oh. Weird.

LOT. Do you know that one?

GINNY. I don't like that one.

LOT. Okay.

>   *(Pause.)*

GINNY. I have a crush on someone.

LOT. Who is it?

GINNY. Ben Dickson.

LOT. Who's Ben Dickson?

GINNY. A really cute boy.

LOT. Where'd you meet him?

GINNY. At Special Olympics Bowling.

LOT. Okay congratulations. Does he know you like him?

GINNY. Well he's my boyfriend.

LOT. Okay congratulations.

GINNY. Yeah!

>   *(She's unbearably happy, she does a little*
>   *dance.)*

LOT. What's he like?

GINNY. He's very cute. He's good at bowling. He's fourteen.

LOT. He's fourteen?

GINNY. Yes.

LOT. How old are you?

GINNY. I'm thirty-four.

LOT. Ginny.

GINNY. Yeah.

LOT. Ginny.

GINNY. What?

LOT. You can't.

GINNY. I can't what?

LOT. You're not allowed! Don't you *know* that?

GINNY. Not allowed what? He's my boyfriend.

LOT. No he's not.

GINNY. What?

LOT. Oh no. No – Ginny.

> *(He starts having a panic attack.)*

Sorry. Sorry – I'm sorry. It's gonna get hard for me to speak. Just for a moment.

Sorry sorry sorry sorry.

Sorry sorry sorry.

I'm sorry. It's not a big deal.

Sorry. It's not a big deal.

Sorry. Not a big deal.

Sorry. Not a big deal.

Sorry.

> *(He gets very quiet. He tries to breathe. This takes a long time. Eventually,* **GINNY** *rubs his back. He flinches, moves away.)*

GINNY. Tell me you're okay.

LOT. You just have to be careful, Ginny, okay?

GINNY. About what?

LOT. About who you like. You can't let yourself like the wrong people.

GINNY. Okay. Like who?

LOT. Like Ben Dickson. He's too young. He's just a boy. People don't always know how good you are. They can't always tell.

GINNY. I'm a really good person.

LOT. I bet you are.

GINNY. And Ben is too young, but I'm really good, and he's too young for me, and I'm a grown woman.

LOT. Right.

GINNY. And people need to know that I'm a good person.

LOT. They do.

GINNY. Do they think I'm bad?

LOT. No, but they might just get confused.

GINNY. Well, he's not my boyfriend, and I should not have said that. He's just a volunteer and a cute kid. I need to choose my words carefully.

LOT. I understand.

(He tries to calm down from the panic attack.)

They just don't want what you want to be real. The one thing they never want it to be is real.

GINNY. Yeah. Huh?

LOT. It's not allowed to be real for us. They can't deal with it. They can't let it happen.

GINNY. Who?

LOT. Styrofoam people.

Why would I ever want to be styrofoam? Yeah why would I ever want to be styrofoam? Well because styrofoam people are allowed to *want* things. And if you're special you're just supposed to *need* things.

Styrofoam people get to spend time with their wanting. Yeah they lie in bed at night, wanting something. And they dream about it. And they wake up the next day and say: I'm gonna try to get that thing that I want. And they go around trying to get that thing. Just because they want it.

And then someone like me comes around. Or someone like you comes around. Complicated people. Layered people. Granite. Basalt. Obsidian people. We're so complicated people don't want to think about it. So they make us more simple. In their brains. They don't think about it, and they call us simple. And everything is about our *needs*. All our little *needs*. Our special needs. Everyone around us becoming burdened by our constant need. And if there's something that we want? Well it's for them to decide if we really *need* it.

   (Pause.)

So, what do you – yeah what do you want, Ginny?

GINNY. I don't know.

LOT. Yes you do.

GINNY. I'm fine.

LOT. Tell me what you want.

GINNY. Ice cream.

LOT. I don't have that.

GINNY. We can go get it. It needs to be fat-free and dairy-free.

LOT. I'm not talking about ice cream.

GINNY. I know.

LOT. I'm talking about what you *want*.

GINNY. I know.

LOT. So tell me.

GINNY. Maybe a Sprite.

> (**GINNY** *laughs.* **LOT** *laughs for the first time –*
> *it bursts out of him strangely.*)

Fine. I want a new birthday. Because it's too close to Christmas. And a new family.

LOT. Okay!

GINNY. More of a family. I want a family in California. With lots of pop stars and special kids.

LOT. Great. What else do you want?

GINNY. I want a boyfriend to become a husband. And I want to become a mom.

LOT. Right.

GINNY. And have five blonde kids.

LOT. Okay.

GINNY. And six blonde boyfriends.

LOT. At the same time.

GINNY. Yep. But only one husband. With curly brown hair.

> (**LOT** *laughs again.* **GINNY** *laughs.*)

I just want a different life. And a different house. And a new smile.

LOT. No, your smile is fine.

GINNY. Not really. And people will give it to me, because my mom passed away.

LOT. People will give it to you?

GINNY. She left it in her will.

LOT. She left you a new smile in her will?

GINNY. A new life. I think so.

LOT. Oh. What was it like when your mom died?

GINNY. Hey, stop. I don't know.

LOT. Okay.

(Pause.)

GINNY. We were having a birthday party, it was my birthday party, I was thirty-four years old and my mom was ready in the kitchen to give a big speech about me and before I know it Justice says *oh my God, Leanne, Leanne, I need help, somebody call an ambulance, somebody call an ambulance* and I had no idea what was going on. And the little kids were driving me insane being noisy and disrespectful so I actually slapped a child in the face because I was worried about my mom. And the ambulance came and they could not wake her up and I said *Mom, Mom please wake up* and she would not wake up and later I had to say goodbye. But I feel bad for losing my temper because I should not do that.

LOT. Yeah. That's bad.

GINNY. Oh, that's okay. Because she's happy for me, and checking in on me.

LOT. Good.

GINNY. Because I do have a boyfriend. His name is Tim and he's thirty-five years old. He's a prankster. He actually got water in his brain. He calls me way too much. But he touched my bottom when I asked him not to.

LOT. He did what?

GINNY. Yeah.

(She buries her face in her hands.)

LOT. Oh no. Ginny. He shouldn't have done that. Okay? He should not have done that. You asked him not to.

GINNY. People have to understand touch, and ask for permission, and respect boundaries.

LOT. Yes.

GINNY. Touch can cause problems. And when I said that my brother Christopher touched me, he got in trouble. I was trying to understand the lesson about touch. It wasn't his fault or my fault but it made him cry and get upset.

LOT. Your brother touched you?

GINNY. It was my mistake. About choosing words carefully.

LOT. Ginny, you're confusing me.

GINNY. Oh, don't worry. I'm just getting things off my chest. I need to talk everything out.

>   (**LOT** *stares at the ground.* **GINNY** *puts her hand on his back. He jerks away from her.)*

I love you.

LOT. What? Stop it. You're confusing me.

GINNY. Oh, that's okay. I love you.

>   (**LOT** *stands up. He spits.)*

LOT. Sorry.

GINNY. Ew.

LOT. Sorry.

>   (*He walks outside. He walks back inside.)*

GINNY. Are you okay?

LOT. Shut up for a second. Just shut up.

>   (*Now:)*

>   (**JUSTICE** *and* **CHRISTOPHER** *are in Lot's house.* **LOT** *is very upset.)*

This was a bad idea. It's hopeless. I'm done.

JUSTICE. Don't say that, Lot.

LOT. I'm the one who's doing it, I'm the one who knows.

JUSTICE. But we're telling you it's not hopeless.

LOT. You don't know that.

JUSTICE. Neither do you.

CHRISTOPHER. Look I just feel bad.

LOT. Leave me alone all of you, I'm done.

CHRISTOPHER. Okay if that's how you feel –

JUSTICE. No, Christopher, stay for a minute, let's –

LOT. I'm done.

CHRISTOPHER. Yeah, oh man, and look I'm sorry that it got –

JUSTICE. You're not done, Lot.

LOT. Why?

JUSTICE. Because I think it's good for you.

LOT. It's not good for me. You can't just say it's good for me and make it true just by saying it.

JUSTICE. Okay I'm sorry, I thought you said it *was* –

LOT. I changed my mind. That's allowed! It's not good for me it's bad for me. It's hurting me.

CHRISTOPHER. Oh man, I'm so sorry…

LOT. I told you to leave.

JUSTICE. Christopher, stay. Lot, what's hurting you about it?

LOT. All of it.

JUSTICE. I want you to be more specific.

LOT. I don't want to be more specific.

JUSTICE. Well you need to be – so that I understand and so that Christopher understands.

LOT. It just hurts. Every second of it hurts me. I'm supposed to help her make a song, well why?

She doesn't want to make a song. I'm supposed to spend all this time with her, well why?

She doesn't want to spend time with me.

JUSTICE. She does – she told us that she does. You're projecting, you're reading into things –

CHRISTOPHER. She really does, she's been talking about you nonstop at home –

LOT. I'm bad for her.

JUSTICE. Why are you bad for her?

LOT. Just am.

JUSTICE. Christopher, do you think Lot is good for her?

CHRISTOPHER. Yeah I do, in my opinion.

JUSTICE. And I think so too, and Ginny thinks so too. And if you'd let us bring her in here, she could tell you herself.

LOT. No, don't bring her in here.

JUSTICE. Okay, and why is that?

LOT. I don't want to be around her.

JUSTICE. And why is that?

LOT. I just don't.

JUSTICE. You agreed to do this, don't be a quitter.

LOT. Your word, not mine.

JUSTICE. Was there a thing that happened?

LOT. What do you mean?

JUSTICE. Lot, Ginny called me crying and saying that you were upset at her, so I want you to tell me what happened.

LOT. Nothing happened.

JUSTICE. Nothing happened.

LOT. FINE. Know what it is? I don't know what to do with a goddamn thing she says. She tells me people touch her. Says her own brother touched her. What am I supposed to say to that?

CHRISTOPHER. What?

JUSTICE. She –

CHRISTOPHER. She said that?

> (**GINNY** *comes in.*)

GINNY. What's taking so long?

LOT. Ginny, out.

GINNY. I actually need to use the bathroom –

LOT. GET OUT OF HERE.

GINNY. Excuse me?

LOT. IT WAS SUPPOSED TO MAKE ME FEEL BRAVE.

PEOPLE WERE SUPPOSED TO START COMING IN.

I DON'T FEEL BRAVE. I FEEL AFRAID. SO GET THE FUCK OUT.

JUSTICE. LOT – STOP IT!

LOT. WHY ARE YOU DOING THIS TO ME JUSTICE?

JUSTICE. WHAT AM I DOING?

CHRISTOPHER. Ginny maybe we should uh –

GINNY. What did I do?

> (**GINNY** *has started to pee her pants. She runs to the bathroom.*)

Okay now I'm embarrassed.

CHRISTOPHER. Oh man –

JUSTICE. Oh honey –

> (**JUSTICE** *goes to help* **GINNY**. **CHRISTOPHER**
> *and* **LOT** *sit in a long silence. Finally:*)

CHRISTOPHER. I can't believe she –

Just so you, uh – I just... I should say that, uh, oh my
God...

> (*After a big sigh:*)

It was when we were in high school. It was a
misunderstanding. She was learning about inappropriate
touch in school. They kept talking about it. They were
teaching them about not touching *here* and *here*.

> (*He reluctantly demonstrates touch on the
> chest and touch on the groin.*)

And she went to her teacher and said I touched her there
and there. I don't know why. Because of hugs? Because
hugs can technically touch those places. Or because we
slept in the same bed when we were kids. I don't know.
That was the worst day of my life. Well, and I'm sorry if
that threw you off. She just... she's really, she just...

> (**LOT** *just stares at the ground.*)

God. Just, sorry if...

> (**GINNY** *comes back. She tries to give* **LOT** *a hug.*
> *He jerks away – it feels scary.* **CHRISTOPHER**
> *whispers something in* **GINNY***'s ear. She looks*
> *at him.*)

GINNY. Seriously? I give up.

> (**CHRISTOPHER** *and* **GINNY** *leave.* **JUSTICE**
> *looks at* **LOT***, who's catatonic.*)

JUSTICE. Don't go down into wherever it is you're going.

>   *(Pause.)*

Or do, I guess. What do I know.

>   *(Pause.)*

Anyhow, you're not alone. And I felt like things were going pretty okay, for a second. So I don't know what happened. But if you want to talk, I'm here.

>   *(Pause.)*

You working on something new back there? I saw that new thing.

Looks like a mountain. Looks like a whole planet.

You're building a whole Earth in there?

LOT. *(Snapping.)* You're not supposed to look back there.

JUSTICE. Hello.

LOT. Anything I make is a one-way street to God. Then God does whatever He wants with it. It's not for you it's not for me it's just for God. And I'm not your project. I'm nobody's project but God. And when I die it'll be God who takes it all up into Him, not those kids, not the lady with the notepad, not the magazines, not the frames, not you and not me. Just God. So don't look back there. And don't think of me, not ever again. Leave.

>   *(Pause. Eventually* **JUSTICE** *exhales.)*

JUSTICE. Well. So. I'll come by tomorrow.

LOT. No. You're never coming back here.

JUSTICE. Lot. No. That can't be what this is. How is that what this is?

>   *(He's done talking. It takes her a while to move. Eventually, she leaves.)*

(Now:)

*(**LOT** is by the gate at the front of his property.)*

(He swings it shut.)

(He wraps the chain.)

(He locks the padlock.)

End of Part One

Part Two

[MUSIC #4 – THIS IS MY LOVE SONG]

(A sleek and sexy pop music beat. The beat drops. **GINNY** *emerges in a swirl of glory.)*

GINNY. *(Singing and dancing.)*
YEAH YEAH YEAH
OH YEAH YEAH YEAH YEAH
OH OH OH
OH YEAH

THIS IS MY CHANCE
OH YEAH YEAH YEAH YEAH
THIS IS MY LOVE SONG
YEAH YEAH YEAH

THIS IS MY
OH YEAH
THE WAY YOU
THIS IS MY
YEAH YEAH YEAH

(The lights are suddenly stripped away. **GINNY** *is alone in her den. She looks at her iPad. She screams.)*

THE INTERNET STOPPED WORKING. CHRISTOPHER!

THE INTERNET STOPPED WORKING. Oh, I hate this.

*(**CHRISTOPHER** comes on. He goes to the router. He unplugs every cable from the router. He waits. Yawns. He plugs all the wires back in. Waits.)*

CHRISTOPHER. Hm.

GINNY. Is it working?

CHRISTOPHER. Not yet.

(She checks her iPad. It's not working.)

GINNY. This is so frustrating.

CHRISTOPHER. Just give me a second.

GINNY. I hate this.

CHRISTOPHER. I know.

GINNY. What do we do?

CHRISTOPHER. I'll call EarthLink.

GINNY. Please fix it. Please.

CHRISTOPHER. Okay I have to go to work, though. What are you gonna do today?

GINNY. I don't know.

CHRISTOPHER. Maybe I'll call Justice.

GINNY. No I'm fine.

CHRISTOPHER. Well you can't just watch movies and drink soda all day.

GINNY. Well I'm FINE with that. I make my own decisions.

CHRISTOPHER. I know.

GINNY. Actually I'm older than you.

CHRISTOPHER. I know.

GINNY. And a lot of people depend on me. Like friends. The whole town. And I want to see them.

CHRISTOPHER. So let me take you to see them. Let's call them.

GINNY. No, forget about it.

CHRISTOPHER. Why not?

GINNY. No one takes me to see them. Mom takes me to see them.

CHRISTOPHER. Well now I have to be the one to take you.

GINNY. But I don't get excited about it anymore. Because Lot didn't like me. And actually, nobody likes me.

CHRISTOPHER. No, Ginny, that was just... that was complicated. Lot's just –

GINNY. It's not just Lot. Because no one talks to me every single night. I can't remember my Facebook password.

CHRISTOPHER. I know. I'm sorry. I know. I tried everything. I couldn't remember it. And I can't remember your email password to reset it. But you don't have to be on Facebook to talk to people.

GINNY. Whatever.

*(Unseen, **JUSTICE** comes into the kitchen with groceries.)*

CHRISTOPHER. Ginny? I think maybe we should find someone for you to talk to.

GINNY. Like who?

CHRISTOPHER. Like a therapist or someone.

GINNY. No, are you kidding me? You have to think of something different.

CHRISTOPHER. Okay well how do I do that? If you don't help me come up with ideas.

GINNY. I'm older than you.

CHRISTOPHER. Ginny, I know!

GINNY. I'm older than you, I'm the older sister, and I know how to take care of this family.

CHRISTOPHER. I know –

GINNY. So leave me alone. Jerk. Bitch.

CHRISTOPHER. Ginny, I just don't want you to be –

GINNY. Bitch.

> *(She storms off and slams the door. From behind the door, we hear her screaming.* **CHRISTOPHER** *stands there. Then he turns and sees* **JUSTICE** *in the kitchen.)*

JUSTICE. Sorry, didn't want to interrupt.

CHRISTOPHER. What am I doing wrong?

JUSTICE. Nothing, honey. Nothing at all. What do you need?

CHRISTOPHER. *(Putting his wrists on his hips.)* I don't need anything. I can handle it. I'm sorry to make you do so much.

JUSTICE. You're not making me do a thing. Look at you, wrists on your hips, exactly like your mom. Look –

> *(She shows him a picture of Leanne on her phone.)*

CHRISTOPHER. *(Dropping his hands.)* I didn't even notice.

JUSTICE. It's a good thing. Okay I had a thought. Ready?

CHRISTOPHER. Yeah?

JUSTICE. Get away from here. Go see some of your friends. Yeah? Go up to Dallas. I can stay here.

CHRISTOPHER. Really?

JUSTICE. Really.

CHRISTOPHER. Wow. That didn't even occur to me.

JUSTICE. There's a whole world out there.

CHRISTOPHER. I mean my friend did invite me to his ranch. His family has a – but I shouldn't, I don't want to run away.

JUSTICE. Taking some time to yourself isn't running away.

CHRISTOPHER. Okay. Yeah. Thanks. Maybe. But I really do think I can get things feeling good here again. But thanks. But, uh, how are you?

JUSTICE. How am I?

CHRISTOPHER. How are you?

JUSTICE. How am I? How am I?

How am I? How am I?

How am I?

CHRISTOPHER. Yeah what's happening right now? How are you?

> *(Now:)*
>
> *(**JUSTICE** goes to Lot's gate. It's locked. She looks at it.)*
>
> *(Now:)*
>
> *(**CHRISTOPHER** comes in. Drunk. **GINNY** on the couch. She's holding pencils and tapping them against a DVD case.)*

CHRISTOPHER. You pencil tapping?

GINNY. Yes.

CHRISTOPHER. You haven't done that in so long.

GINNY. Oh well I do love it.

CHRISTOPHER. One Christmas I just got you a box of pencils. Oh do you remember that little movie I made about it for my film elective? I was like sixteen.

GINNY. Oh I forgot.

CHRISTOPHER. It was called *Pencil Tapper*. Why'd I do that in black and white? Pretentious.

(After a beat:)

Are you still mad at me?

GINNY. No, just frustrated.

CHRISTOPHER. I'm frustrated too. I don't like fighting. I got a little drunk.

GINNY. Oh boy.

(He sits down next to her.)

CHRISTOPHER. I'm sorry I'm really bad at being a caretaker.

GINNY. I'm a caretaker too.

CHRISTOPHER. I know you are.

GINNY. And a caregiver.

CHRISTOPHER. Right. Yeah. I have a headache. I feel awful.

GINNY. It's not good to drink too much beer.

CHRISTOPHER. It was mezcal.

GINNY. Yeah, see?

CHRISTOPHER. Okay. I just want you to know that I love you a lot. You're my full sister.

GINNY. I'm your half-sister.

CHRISTOPHER. I'm saying that you feel like my full sister.

GINNY. No, I'm your older half-sister.

CHRISTOPHER. I know. Nevermind.

GINNY. Because we're not exactly the same, actually. We're different.

CHRISTOPHER. Yeah well the part of you that's a part of me is *her*, and that's my favorite part of me.

GINNY. Huh?

CHRISTOPHER. Whatever.

GINNY. Stop pushing me away.

CHRISTOPHER. What?

GINNY. You're pushing me away.

CHRISTOPHER. No I'm not.

GINNY. I didn't do anything wrong.

CHRISTOPHER. I didn't say you did.

GINNY. You always accuse me of things. I'm not lazy or sneaking soda and I'm healthy and fat-free and dairy-free and I'm taking care of my body by myself. So don't accuse me.

CHRISTOPHER. I wasn't accusing you of anything, Ginny!

GINNY. Yes you were. Because I don't need you to tell me what to do. I need you to help me as a brother who knows about me. Not to give me rules. I know the life that I need to have, and nobody is letting me have that.

CHRISTOPHER. Okay, well me neither!

GINNY. Well I know that!

CHRISTOPHER. I have things I want to make. And I want to date someone. I haven't been touched in like a year and a half.

GINNY. Touch is complicated. So you need to be careful with that.

CHRISTOPHER. Yeah, well, Ginny, you know what? I was really hurt when you told Lot that I touched you. That was really, really hard to hear, because you told me that was a misunderstanding –

GINNY. I know it was a misunderstanding, and that's what I said. I said that to him. Okay? So don't be upset because I understand better now. And you learned how to be better too.

CHRISTOPHER. No, I didn't learn anything, because I didn't do anything. It was only confusing. All I learned was that you know *exactly* how to, just, destroy me. And that you make things up.

GINNY. No I don't. It's about choosing words –

CHRISTOPHER. And that it's impossible, it's just impossible and everything I do is wrong. You're so *mean* to me all the time.

GINNY. What?

CHRISTOPHER. You are. You're being mean to me. I'm trying really hard and you're being mean.

> *(Pause.)*

GINNY. Well, I did not intend... oh man I hate this. I did not intend to be mean or rude to you. Come here.

> *(She hugs him.)*

I apologize. From the bottom of my heart.

CHRISTOPHER. I apologize too.

GINNY. You've got edge, bro. You've got issues.

CHRISTOPHER. Bro don't even start.

> *(They sit there.)*

GINNY. Because I'm doing my best.

CHRISTOPHER. I know. Me too. Is it okay that I'm going away this weekend?

GINNY. It's fine. But I want to go out of town too.

CHRISTOPHER. Yeah.

> *(Pause.)*

Would you ever want to move to California?

GINNY. Are you serious?

CHRISTOPHER. Yeah. Would you ever wanna act in movies that I made?

GINNY. Are they gonna be good?

CHRISTOPHER. I hope so?

GINNY. Okay. Can I sing? Like *High School Musical*?

CHRISTOPHER. I mean I don't really like musicals.

GINNY. Oh, are you serious. Grow up.

CHRISTOPHER. Hahaha

GINNY. Hahaha

CHRISTOPHER. I want to make movies again I think. And like really try.

GINNY. Are you kidding me right now?

CHRISTOPHER. About what?

GINNY. You're making a movie with me.

CHRISTOPHER. Maybe. One day. But like how the heck are we gonna go to California? We couldn't even write one song here. I was gonna make a music video for you.

GINNY. Well you can, because I do things for myself. And I can make the song.

CHRISTOPHER. You can?

GINNY. Yeah.

CHRISTOPHER. You promise?

GINNY. I'll make the song and then we can get famous and go to California.

> (**CHRISTOPHER** *laughs and then gets really sad.*)

CHRISTOPHER. I don't know what I'm so afraid of.

GINNY. It's okay to be scared of the devil.

CHRISTOPHER. I'm not scared of the devil.

GINNY. You should be. When I get afraid, I get sad, or afraid to leave the room, or leave the bed. And it's okay to be scared of the devil at night, or afraid of getting sunburned.

CHRISTOPHER. Sunburned?

GINNY. Just from the sun. Because you're pale, bro. And we can do things for ourselves. In separate houses.

CHRISTOPHER. You don't want to live with me?

GINNY. Not really. I want to live with Zac Efron.

CHRISTOPHER. Okay fine.

GINNY. That's a deal.

> *(They shake on it. He gets up. Starts puttering around the kitchen. Chugs some Pedialyte. She starts tapping pencils again, rewriting the conversation under her breath.)*

(Whispered.) "California?"

"Yes, California."

"Are you serious?"

"Yes. I am. If you write that song."

"I see."

> *(Now:)*

> *(**CHRISTOPHER** gets home. He's a little drunk. **JUSTICE** is watching TV with **GINNY**.)*

JUSTICE. Hey, there he is. How was it?

GINNY. Hey buddy-o.

CHRISTOPHER. Who's buddy-o?

GINNY. That's you.

JUSTICE. How was your friends?

CHRISTOPHER. They were okay. Yeah. They're not a very good influence on me. I love them.

JUSTICE. And the ranch?

CHRISTOPHER. Really cool actually, yeah. They've got a really good – it's a cool ranch.

GINNY. Okay are we talking about Doritos?

> *(They laugh.* **CHRISTOPHER** *sits down between them. They watch the movie.***)*

CHRISTOPHER. Is that Mariah Carey?

JUSTICE. I don't think so.

GINNY. Yes it is.

JUSTICE. Oh.

CHRISTOPHER. Is this a VHS?

GINNY. Yes it is.

CHRISTOPHER. DVD player still not working?

GINNY. No it's not.

> *(They watch.)*

CHRISTOPHER. Is this that movie *Glitter*?

GINNY. Yup.

CHRISTOPHER. Is the Roku not working?

GINNY. The internet is still not working.

CHRISTOPHER. Seriously?

GINNY. Seriously.

---

* A license to produce *CORSICANA* does not include a performance license for any third-party or copyrighted recordings or images. Licensees must acquire rights for any copyrighted recordings or images or create their own.

CHRISTOPHER. Jeez. I called EarthLink and the bill is definitely paid. So I guess someone has to come look at it.

GINNY. That would be great.

CHRISTOPHER. Everything's breaking. My phone's barely getting service. Our house is a black hole.

> *(He gets up to get water.* **JUSTICE** *follows him to the kitchen.* **CHRISTOPHER** *finds a manuscript on the table.)*

What's this?

JUSTICE. Oh that's nothing. Just something I'm writing.

CHRISTOPHER. You're writing something?

JUSTICE. I'm always writing something.

CHRISTOPHER. You are? Is it fiction?

JUSTICE. Not really. It's about anarchism.

CHRISTOPHER. Oh. Are you an anarchist?

JUSTICE. Yes.

CHRISTOPHER. Nuh-uh.

JUSTICE. Yeah-huh.

CHRISTOPHER. Whoa. Cool. What's like, the... what's the like...

> *(**JUSTICE** puts her hand on the manuscript. She sits down.)*

JUSTICE. Well it's about anarchism and gifts. About the belief that humans are fundamentally generous, or at least cooperative. That in our hearts, most of us really do want the good. It's about the evils of centralized power, especially in a country as massive as the USA, let alone a state as big as Texas. It's about an unforgiving land. It's about unrealized utopias. It's about how failing is the point. It's about surrender. It's about small groups. It's about community. It's about the right to well-being. It's about family. It's about the dead. It's about ghosts. It's about gentle chaos. It's about contracts of the heart. And the belief that when a part of the self is given away, is surrendered to the needs of a particular time, in a particular place, then community forms. From the ghosts of the parts of ourselves we've given away. A new particular body. Born of our own ghosts. I don't know. It's about Texas.

CHRISTOPHER. Oh.

JUSTICE. Yeah.

CHRISTOPHER. Justice, we should hang out more. As adults.

JUSTICE. We should.

(**CHRISTOPHER** *nods and then sits down.*)

CHRISTOPHER. Hey, uh, Justice.

JUSTICE. What's up?

CHRISTOPHER. I think I have to go away for a little bit. Again. For like a week. I'm so sorry.

JUSTICE. Oh yeah? Everything okay?

CHRISTOPHER. Yeah everything's okay, yeah, just… yeah my dad's dying.

JUSTICE. What?

CHRISTOPHER. I know. Ridiculous.

JUSTICE. Is it the –

CHRISTOPHER. It's the – yeah, the dialysis just isn't – yeah.

JUSTICE. Oh, Christopher. Jesus Christ. I'm so sorry. Does Ginny know?

CHRISTOPHER. Yeah I told her last, uh – and I'll fly her out if… yeah.

JUSTICE. Oh my God. So you're going to Boulder?

CHRISTOPHER. No he lives in New Mexico now.

JUSTICE. Since when?

CHRISTOPHER. Like three years.

JUSTICE. That man. I can't keep up.

CHRISTOPHER. Yeah he went there to go be super-Christian, and... yeah his super-Christian other son told me it's like one bad day away from hospice and I asked if I should come and he was like "I don't know," but I don't know, I'm reading between the lines and I'm thinking – I'm thinking yeah I should.

JUSTICE. This is too much. This is too much for a person.

CHRISTOPHER. Yeah, but – actually, a lot of interesting things have been happening.

JUSTICE. Like what?

CHRISTOPHER. It's hard to talk about. It's weird.

JUSTICE. Try me.

CHRISTOPHER. Okay. Uh. Like, I found this letter...

JUSTICE. You found a letter?

CHRISTOPHER. I found a letter, yeah. I was trying to build a desk. You know, I've been pretty depressed.

Like – yeah, this has been just a pretty depressing house to live in.

JUSTICE. Yeah. It's my favorite house ever. But I hear you.

CHRISTOPHER. Just, okay, yeah, you know when you told me to go see my friends it really woke me up. Since then, I've been trying to pull myself out of...all this. And really stare it down. Stare my fears down. Or the – I don't know. And I've been trying to meditate or um – pray. And I've been trying to do little exercises. And I was

building this desk... I ordered a desk from Target.com
and I was trying to build it. But I couldn't find a hammer
or screwdriver. And I was looking everywhere for a
hammer or screwdriver. And I couldn't find them. And
I was looking in like a box... like a box of things that
were important to me, things to remember, you know?

JUSTICE. Yes.

GINNY. I can't hear the movie.

CHRISTOPHER. Oh, sorry, Ginny.

JUSTICE. Sorry, Ginny.

(They talk at a quieter volume.)

Okay, so you found a box of things to remember.

CHRISTOPHER. Yeah I found a box of things to remember.
And I was looking through it, and there were all these
things. Like weird mementos, and poems from my
ex-girlfriend, et cetera. And then I find this envelope.

And it's addressed to me, in my mom's handwriting.

And it's addressed to my old address, in Denton.

And I'm like "what's this letter." I don't remember
receiving this letter.

And I open it and I recognize immediately what it is.
It's an apology letter *I* wrote, to my parents when I was
like fifteen, and they were still together. I started getting
obsessed with film that year, and I was watching as
many movies as I could... I would get all these movies
from the library –

JUSTICE. I remember.

CHRISTOPHER. Oh my gosh – yes! You'd –

JUSTICE. I would order the movies we didn't have from
the Dallas library –

CHRISTOPHER. Yes! Even the R-rated ones. You were my
hero. So I would bike over there and get these movies,
and watch them late at night. I was watching everything
on the IMDb Top 250. My grades were tanking but
I didn't care – I was in love. But I was really close to
finishing the IMDb Top 250, but there were a few that
weren't available at the library. Like *12 Monkeys* I think
and *Once Upon a Time in the West* and this Danish
movie *Festen*. And I didn't know what to do, so I stole
my dad's credit card and signed up for Netflix, uh,
subscription, but just the two-week free trial, because
I thought that I could just watch everything in two
weeks, like be the first to check the mail everyday and
get the DVDs and mail them back and then cancel the
subscription and he would never know. And so I did it –
and then I canceled it, and I thought I got away with
it. But I guess they charged him for something anyway.
And he saw it on his statement. And he got really really
mad at me. And this was around the same time that
Ginny said that thing about me touching her. And my
dad had been the one to take me into the school, to
talk to them, and I'd sobbed in front of him, in front
of everyone, and said it wasn't true. And he believed
me. They all did, I think. But then with this Netflix
thing, and me lying, it's like it put everything in a new
light. And I remember that he was really mad at me,
and I remember, as punishment, I was repainting the
kitchen walls – I was painting them that yellow that
they still are over there – I was stripping the masking
tape from the walls – and I remember that I was really
obsessed with *label makers* at the time. My dad had
a label maker and I would write out funny labels and
put them on things. It was a phase I was in. And there
was one that was like "I am Superman" – a label I'd
made that said "I am Superman" – everyone thought
it was funny because I would put it, like, on the fridge
or the toilet – it was an ongoing bit – but like – okay
after I had done this bad thing with Netflix, and I was

doing my punishment and painting the walls, I took the masking tape from the walls and I rolled it all into a ball – and I put the "I am Superman" label on it and gave it to them – along with that apology letter – and I gave them these two things as like an offering – and that "I am Superman" tape thing sat on his Bookshelf of Special Things forever...and when he moved out, he took it with him...

JUSTICE. Wow.

CHRISTOPHER. So everything I just told you was like... *what I remembered.*

And then I found the letter.

And in the letter, basically, I was reading it, and it was like – And this was just like...last week. And I knew that my dad was sick. And that I might have to go see him. And I've been so afraid of that. Did you know I started going to therapy?

JUSTICE. You did? Christopher, that's big.

CHRISTOPHER. But I thought I was going there to talk about my mom, but it's ended up being so much about my dad. Knowing that he's my only parent left. Knowing that I'd have to see him, probably, soon, and feeling so afraid of that. And like – *why*?

JUSTICE. Right.

CHRISTOPHER. And so that was all the context while I was looking for this hammer. In the box.

And I find the letter. And I'm like...Mom sent this to me? When I was in Denton?

Because I don't remember receiving this at all.

Not at all. And it's postmarked and everything. And it's opened.

And it's like – when did she send this? Why don't I remember this?

CHRISTOPHER. And I open it and I read it. And it's just immediately like...wow. Dropping into a moment.

So much detail. Like my fifteen-year-old self is time-traveling, giving me this gift. You know?

JUSTICE. Yeah.

CHRISTOPHER. Does that make sense?

JUSTICE. It does. What did the letter say?

CHRISTOPHER. Well it's like "Dear Mom and Dad" and then it like launches into this overwritten description of a dream I was having, and then this sort of treatise on the nature of dreams... very overwritten and dramatic. But then I'm woken up out of the dream by my dad shouting "GET OUT OF BED." And then I meet him in the hallway and he starts hitting me, just pummeling me with blows. I'm writing these real events to my parents as like, a story. And in the letter I describe being afraid of waking Ginny up, because my dad is hitting me and I'm like slamming into her door.

JUSTICE. Oh my God. And you didn't remember this?

CHRISTOPHER. I had no memory of this. I'd pushed it down. I knew he hit me when I was a little kid, but I didn't know it happened so late. So then...I describe, like...seeing my mom in her room, just silently making the bed. Seeing her and how she knows this is happening, and this cold look on her face.

And then I describe, like...standing in the hallway, shirtless, my face all red from the beating, wearing corduroy pants that have holes in them, because they would get stuck in the bike wheel when I rode my bike to get movies at the library. And then eventually I go back into my room and I'm all sorrowful. And it's only then that the blows start hurting. And I'm like "maybe I'll just never leave my room." And I start writing this letter to my parents.

And it's like a confessional – like everything I've ever done wrong, I list it for them in the letter...and I'm like "I'm going to be a good person, I promise." And "I believe in God, I promise."

And thank you for giving me so much shame.

And thank you for being so hard on me.

And thank you for hitting me.

JUSTICE. Oh, Christopher...

CHRISTOPHER. Yeah and I'm reading this and I'm like... okay well first of all, it makes so much sense that I'm afraid to go see my dad. I'm literally afraid of him. My body is afraid of him.

JUSTICE. Right.

CHRISTOPHER. And second of all, feeling all this gratitude.

JUSTICE. To your mom?

CHRISTOPHER. Oh –

JUSTICE. For sending the letter.

CHRISTOPHER. Oh. Oh. I was gonna – I mean, yes. But no I was gonna say gratitude to my past self, for writing everything down so accurately. *So* accurately – literally giving this gift to my future self.

JUSTICE. I see. Yes.

CHRISTOPHER. The memory came back intact. Right when I needed it most.

JUSTICE. Yes. I see.

CHRISTOPHER. So then I mentioned this letter up in therapy, of course. And she's like "bring that letter to the next session." So I'm like "okay." So that was last Monday, and then I went to the ranch with my friends this weekend, and we got back late this morning, and I went right to Navarro, and then therapy was right after. And then I had to get a drink.

JUSTICE. Right. Okay. What happened? Oh my God.

CHRISTOPHER. Okay I'm just going to tell you, okay: I did shrooms with my friends at the ranch.

JUSTICE. Mushrooms?

CHRISTOPHER. Yeah, please don't judge me... it's actually like really safe, and it's such a wonderful drug, it's like the best drug. It's from the earth. It connects you to everything that's alive on the earth.

JUSTICE. Oh Christopher. Trust me, I know.

CHRISTOPHER. Oh. Haha, oh.

JUSTICE. Was it your first time?

CHRISTOPHER. Yeah, it was. It's amazing!

JUSTICE. Yes. Oh that's so good. Good.

CHRISTOPHER. Okay wow so okay I went into the weekend thinking I would tell my friends about this letter. Like, hey guys want to see the most important object in my life? But I didn't, I just never did. I kept it in my backpack. Instead, I drink this mushroom, like, tea?, that my friend made. And eventually I started having this incredible experience, where I was half-myself and half-my-dad. Like, I literally felt like half of my body was his. But like when he was my age. So half of me was this football-playing Christian in the 70s, and half of me was an out-of-shape failed filmmaker today. And it was the wildest thing – I got really adventurous. I had to like run everywhere and touch everything. And I felt really like...masculine. And really invested in performing a certain type of masculinity. But then the me-side of myself was really ashamed that I was doing that. Like super embarrassed that I was running around and touching things and being so masculine... but then half of me was like "I have to do this."

And it was this insane act of understanding him.

Understanding what it was like to be inside his body. And to care about the things that he cared about. And to not be able to transfer that way of being into his son. It must have driven him crazy. And that just is what it is. And I forgive him. And that feels complicated and good.

JUSTICE. You seem better. You seem brighter.

CHRISTOPHER. I do?

JUSTICE. You do. Aw, I wanna do shrooms.

CHRISTOPHER. Oh my gosh we should totally do them together. Can we?

JUSTICE. Let's do it.

CHRISTOPHER. Let's find a time and do it. Hahaha. That would be crazy. But I'm into it.

JUSTICE. Me too. It's been too long. I've been desperate for a numinous experience. As I approach the second half of the second half of my life.

CHRISTOPHER. Well I think this could be that. Okay so, but…sorry okay so I came back today and I was going to therapy. I brought the letter to therapy like she asked. And I was a little early so I went to McDonald's right next door. And I was in McDonald's reading the letter.

And then I was like, oops, time to go to therapy. So I put the letter in my jacket pocket, on the inside, and walked over there.

And then inside the building, the elevator was taking a long time. Like a really long time, like stopping at every floor. And I was like: *that's weird. So long at every floor. What an elevator mystery.* And then it finally came down and a postal worker came out, like a mailwoman… And I was like ohhh of course. That's the answer to the riddle. That's why an elevator would stop so long at every floor. Mystery solved.

CHRISTOPHER. And then I walked into therapy and I was like "I brought the letter." And she was like "great." And I reach into my jacket pocket and…it's gone.

JUSTICE. No!

CHRISTOPHER. It's just gone. And I start freaking out immediately. Like this can't be happening. And she starts freaking out too – and she's like – *go look for it.*

JUSTICE. Oh my God.

CHRISTOPHER. So I retrace my steps and I go back to look for it and it's nowhere to be found.

It's not in McDonald's, it's not in the trash, it's not on the sidewalk on the way over there. It's gone. And I go back to therapy. And I'm like it's gone. And she's like *holy crap.* And I like can't breathe – and I close my eyes tight. And she's like, okay – "just tell me everything you can that was in the letter." And I'm like okay. So I get out my phone and started writing it all out on my Notes app while I'm talking to her. And I try to remember everything I can. But I feel most of it slipping away forever.

> *(He remembers something else from the letter. He gets out his phone and types something into the Notes app.)*

Sorry.

JUSTICE. You remembered something?

CHRISTOPHER. Yeah. Trying not to forget. All the little…

> *(He tries to remember more, but he can't. He sits there, very still.)*

Okay.

JUSTICE. And the letter's just gone?

CHRISTOPHER. It's just gone. Yeah. I see three options:

One. It fell out on the street and was taken by the wind or thrown away as garbage, because who could have known how important it was, because a letter is just paper.

Two. Pickpockets – unlikely but possible, I did walk through a small grouping of young men on my way out of McDonald's.

Three. And this is my preference: It was taken by the postal worker, who was actually an angel – because remember the letter appeared to me mysteriously, addressed to me by my mom, who's dead, and who I keep dreaming about – and the letter vanished as mysteriously as it appeared. So I think she sent it down to me via the United States Postal Service. And then I think she took it back up via the same methods.

Mhm.

(Pause.)

JUSTICE. Christopher?

CHRISTOPHER. Yeah?

JUSTICE. Thank you for that gift.

CHRISTOPHER. What gift?

*(**GINNY** walks up to **CHRISTOPHER**.)*

GINNY. Get your phone, buddy-o.

CHRISTOPHER. What?

GINNY. Your phone.

*(**CHRISTOPHER** gets out his phone.)*

Now film me.

CHRISTOPHER. What is this?

GINNY. Are you filming.

CHRISTOPHER. *(Pressing record.)* Okay, yes.

GINNY. *(To the camera.)* Hi, Dad. This is Ginny. And yes, Daddy-o, you heard that right, because I know you always said "call me Dad," and I could not actually do it because I got upset. Because I did actually know that you were not my blood actual father, and that my mom had some issues and complications with her marriage to you. And how you thought Mom and I were always a team against you. But then you accepted me and took me on, as a daughter. And your son Christopher wants to spend some time with you, to help you to not be sick. And he's a good adult man who helps people feel better. You have a good son, so pray to Jesus to be a good dad, okay? I'm done. I love you.

> *(**CHRISTOPHER** stops filming. **GINNY** touches his nose.)*

Boop.

> *(Now:)*

> *(**CHRISTOPHER** is gone. **JUSTICE** is at the kitchen table. Dishes on it. **GINNY** is cleaning up.)*

I have an idea, actually.

> *(Pause.)*

I have an idea, Justice.

> *(No response. **GINNY** coughs.)*

Justice.

> *(**GINNY** comes over to **JUSTICE**, who looks up finally.)*

Are you okay?

JUSTICE. Yes. Sorry. Sorry.

GINNY. Giving me a heart attack. I thought you were dead.

JUSTICE. No, no. Sorry, no. Just beside myself. Sitting here beside myself. A ghost of myself from the future maybe, sitting here, old and droopy, telling me to do something I'm afraid to do.

GINNY. Sitting here like a ghost?

JUSTICE. Yeah. Don't be scared.

GINNY. You're scared.

JUSTICE. I am but it's okay. It's okay. Just don't sit there. Just sit here. Sit here with me.

> (**GINNY** *sits where* **JUSTICE** *points. There are two empty chairs.)*

GINNY. Is this where the ghost is sitting?

JUSTICE. No, she's not sitting there.

GINNY. Oh man, I hate this.

JUSTICE. It's okay. It's just me. It's just everything at once. Me sitting here with your mom…

GINNY. You and my mom are ghosts at this table? I hate that.

JUSTICE. And there's a dead man too. It's okay.

GINNY. What dead man? I'm terrified. Three ghosts? This is ridiculous.

JUSTICE. No, it's okay. Sorry. Everyone's happy. Everyone's gentle and nice.

> (*This is a five-person scene.* **JUSTICE**. **GINNY**. *Justice's Ghost. Leanne's Ghost. The Dead Man.)*

GINNY. Are you sure?

JUSTICE. Positive.

GINNY. Just coming to help?

JUSTICE. Exactly. Very helpful.

GINNY. Like how my mom tells me not to do things or how to be good. She comes to me in the night, she sits on my bed. We talk. It's okay, it's not scary.

JUSTICE. Really?

GINNY. Sometimes. And it's okay.

(Pause.)

JUSTICE. She was my best friend.

GINNY. Well I know that.

JUSTICE. She was the funniest person I've ever met in my life.

GINNY. Yep. And she was cranky and bossy.

JUSTICE. Sometimes, yep. She would be making so much fun of me right now.

GINNY. And why is that?

JUSTICE. Because I'm thinking about romantic love, and I told her I would never think about it again. I told her, I swore up and down, we were sitting right here and I told her I. DO NOT. BELIEVE. IN ROMANTIC LOVE. She laughed so hard that she broke the chair. But here I am again. Wanting it. You win, Leanne. But what *is* it? I can't be wanting it again, can I? Why would I want it again? It messed me up wholesale last time. It almost killed me. And it wasn't real, anyway, none of it was real, it was all a brutality and a lie. I am really truly struggling to believe that such love is true and real. I know that I love *you*, and Christopher, and my sisters, and so many goddamn people –

GINNY. I don't like that word.

JUSTICE. Sorry. Sorry. But why does this love for Lot feel different?

GINNY. What? Lot?

JUSTICE. I have a crush on him.

GINNY. Are you kidding me right now?

JUSTICE. Nope. I'm a bozo. I've liked him for a long time.

> (**GINNY** *gives* **JUSTICE** *a big hug.*)

GINNY. Okay, I want to be the Best of Honor.

JUSTICE. The Best of Honor? You mean the Maid of Honor.

GINNY. The Best Maid of Honor.

JUSTICE. Well I don't even know if he likes me back.

GINNY. He does.

JUSTICE. But Ginny I mean this is absurd. This is completely ridiculous. To like him. To love him. But it's not going away. It just gets stronger. I miss him. And yet I have become so deeply cynical. Romantic love. I think that it sounds like an excellent idea in theory, but put into practice it seems nearly impossible. It *is* impossible. I know it is. I already know that I'll fall out of love, because ultimately it's just wanting to be loved and not actually wanting to do the hard work of loving. We retreat back into ourselves. So then you say, what about Rilke, what about two solitudes protecting each other. Okay, that sounds nice, but is it even possible? Don't we just end up eating each other, hating each other, feasting on the hate? It seems like just a simple evolutionary habit, a way of keeping from encountering the self in its full horror.

GINNY. I don't like horror.

JUSTICE. Me neither, but being a person is the most horrifying thing in the world.

GINNY. Well, I actually don't know about that.

JUSTICE. Okay. Fair. Just my opinion.

GINNY. To be a person means to be yourself with God.

JUSTICE. Okay. And that's your opinion.

GINNY. Exactly.

JUSTICE. I look at my parents' love, all of its stubbornness, its hanging-on, despite all the infidelity and silence and abuse, yes okay, they had it for fifty years, but it seemed made up of so much triage and so many labyrinths as to make it almost an optical illusion. And it was a beautiful illusion, but wasn't it just *necessity*? Survival? An octopus changing its color. A marvel of duty and imagination, but nothing actual. Nothing actually *there*. A supreme fiction. Then again, when you see somebody who loves somebody else despite all their flaws and foibles and bullcrap, then I don't know if there's anything better in the whole world. I mean that's just a miracle. Then again, how tragic that we're all trained to believe we deserve a miracle.

GINNY. Well you do.

JUSTICE. Well okay. And then the hardest thing: to allow yourself to be loved knowing all those things about oneself.

GINNY. What things?

JUSTICE. All the horror. All the things. There are so many things wrong with me.

GINNY. Not really.

JUSTICE. There are. Disgusting things. Ridiculous things. I'm a perverted old spy. I'm a hypocrite. I'm a candy-ass.

GINNY. Well, that's okay.

JUSTICE. I really don't think it is. Anyhow, it's too late. He never wants to see me again.

GINNY. Yes, he does.

JUSTICE. No, he doesn't.

GINNY. Well, why not? Did you hurt his feelings?

JUSTICE. I guess so.

GINNY. How?

JUSTICE. I don't know, I guess I...

> *(Pause.)*

Oh no.

GINNY. Do you know what you did?

JUSTICE. I think so. I think I lied to him.

GINNY. Well. It's not difficult to say you're sorry. You just have to say it out loud.

JUSTICE. Yeah. I'm scared.

GINNY. It's gonna be okay.

JUSTICE. I don't know if it is. Why am I this way?

GINNY. What way?

JUSTICE. Afraid to ask for what I want. It makes me sneaky. I give so much to people, and secretly the whole time I try to bend things to my liking. Which makes the giving dishonest.

GINNY. And what do you want?

JUSTICE. I don't know. A failed utopia.

GINNY. And what is that?

JUSTICE. I don't know. A family.

GINNY. Okay. Look at me, I get it. Look at me. I don't know why I am the way I am. But I want a husband and a family and a boyfriend. And I'm scared to be alone. And I have a lot of feelings for people. Feelings in my heart and in my body.

JUSTICE. Right, I know that's hard for you.

GINNY. Just listen to me.

JUSTICE. Okay.

GINNY. Because I do have a body as a woman.

JUSTICE. I know.

GINNY. And desire as a woman.

JUSTICE. Right.

GINNY. And I do believe that I deserve it.

JUSTICE. Of course you deserve it.

GINNY. It is hard to want touch. And to want true love. And to want babies. But my mom sat me down and told me that I wasn't allowed.

JUSTICE. She did?

GINNY. And that was not okay to me.

JUSTICE. I'm sure she was just doing her best.

GINNY. Yes, she was doing her best. It's nobody's fault. But she can't tell me not to want what I want, do you understand?

JUSTICE. Yes.

GINNY. Because I love when two people are in love. It's my favorite thing. Even if it's scary or you think about dying in his arms. Or not having the love in your heart anymore. Or falling off the cliff.

JUSTICE. Okay.

GINNY. And so you have to be brave and stick up for yourself. And be honest. And you have to be with your special heart.

JUSTICE. Okay.

GINNY. And you have to love with a special heart, okay?

JUSTICE. Yes.

GINNY. So tell him. It's the right thing.

JUSTICE. You're right.

GINNY. And if you do it, God will fill your whole body. And give you a new body.

> (**JUSTICE** *gives* **GINNY** *a big hug.*)

And tell him that I need to finish my song.

JUSTICE. You want to finish your song?

GINNY. I have to.

JUSTICE. I don't know if he'll want to.

GINNY. He has to. Okay? It's important. Where's that thing?

> (**GINNY** *finds the tape recorder. She gives it to* **JUSTICE**.)

How does it start?

> (**JUSTICE** *points to the record button.*)

JUSTICE. Ginny, don't say anything about me!

GINNY. Don't worry.

> (**GINNY** *pushes record.*)

Okay turn around.

JUSTICE. *(Turning around.)* Oh okay.

GINNY. Lot, this is for the song. Follow my instructions. You can make the song sort of sad and "waiting around to die" if you want. But it can also be pop, okay? Pop country. And I forgive you. It's nobody's fault. And I miss your heart.

> (*Long pause. She closes her eyes.*)

When I sing to myself, I'm singing just about love.

GINNY. When I sing to myself, it's about love and it's about what I want. I don't know.

When I sing to myself...um. When I sing to myself in my room, I don't want anyone to hear so I sing to myself with the door closed.

Sometimes I forget that I'm capable.

Sometimes I forget to be an adult.

And sometimes I forget that my mom passed away.

And sometimes I remember.

And that's it. Wow, that was bad.

(*To* **JUSTICE**:) Nobody is ever going to hear this song. Nobody is ever allowed to hear this song.

JUSTICE. Should I stop?

GINNY. No. I want to try again –

> (*Now:*)

> (*Lot's house.* **JUSTICE** *walks in.*)

JUSTICE. Lot?

> (*She looks for him.*)

Lot?

> (*She can't find him. She sits down. She waits. A lot of time passes. The light changes.*)

> (*Then* **LOT** *comes in. He sees her there.*)

LOT. How'd you get in here?

JUSTICE. I just came in.

LOT. But the gate was locked.

JUSTICE. I climbed over it, weirdo.

LOT. That's against the law.

JUSTICE. Uh-huh.

LOT. I could get you arrested.

JUSTICE. So call the police.

LOT. I don't have a telephone.

JUSTICE. I know. Where have you been?

LOT. Working.

JUSTICE. Working where?

LOT. The City of Corsicana Regional Landfill.

JUSTICE. You were working at the dump?

LOT. Yes.

JUSTICE. Why?

LOT. I'm employed there.

JUSTICE. You got a job at the dump?

LOT. Yes.

JUSTICE. Why?

LOT. I wanted to.

JUSTICE. But you're opposed to money.

LOT. It's not about the money. I just wanted to work.

JUSTICE. At the dump.

LOT. At the dump yes.

JUSTICE. Oh because you can get your trash there, for your art.

LOT. No I don't take any of it home with me. I'm not making art.

JUSTICE. ...Lot.

LOT. I want to be alone.

JUSTICE. Lot what happened?

LOT. Did you hear me?

JUSTICE. Have you called that woman? Have you checked in about your pieces selling?

LOT. Asked her to send the pieces back. All of them. And she did. They're in a box on the porch.

JUSTICE. Lot. No. Why?

LOT. I read her books. She talks about living men like they're dead. I don't want people getting rich off my purity, which doesn't exist, or my mystery, which doesn't exist.

JUSTICE. Okay. Okay, I hear you. I just... I thought this was what you wanted.

LOT. No, it's what you wanted me to want.

JUSTICE. Is that really what you think?

LOT. Yes it is.

　　　　(Pause.)

JUSTICE. ...Okay. I can see why you thought that.

LOT. You can?

JUSTICE. Yeah. Oh boy. I'm sorry, Lot. You told me all along the way, and I didn't listen. I thought I knew how you felt, better than you did, and... I just... I really feel like scum.

LOT. Well don't, don't feel like scum.

JUSTICE. But it's how I feel.

LOT. Okay then.

JUSTICE. Yeah, and it wasn't just that. There were things that I wanted from you, and I wasn't honest, I was a liar, and I pushed you in a direction you didn't wanna go.

LOT. You did?

JUSTICE. Yeah.

LOT. But I did want something.

JUSTICE. You did?

LOT. Yeah. I told you I wanted to grieve open, not closed. I told you that.

JUSTICE. Well I took it too far. Patronizing. Manipulative. I'm so sorry.

LOT. No. Stop being weird.

(*Pause.*)

I should tell you, uh. So. Yeah I found the root of it upon reflection. And upon reflection what happened was Ginny said she "loved" me.

JUSTICE. Oh...yeah? And that upset you?

LOT. Guess so.

JUSTICE. I'm sure she meant it as a friend.

LOT. It's just the whole idea. What do I do – say it back? And then what? It messes everything up.

(*Pause.*)

JUSTICE. Yeah. That must have been confusing to you. With your history.

LOT. What history?

JUSTICE. When you got kicked out of high school.

LOT. What'd you just say? I never, uh – who told you that?

JUSTICE. Sorry, it's just something I know.

LOT. How do you know things?

JUSTICE. I've lived in this town all my life.

LOT. Well, someone must have told you.

JUSTICE. Fine, the warthog, my ex-husband, he remembered you from the police station.

LOT. He was one of them who took me in?

JUSTICE. He was.

LOT. Yeah. Okay. Yeah. The warthog. Yeah. Sure. So?

JUSTICE. So nothing. Sorry.

LOT. I'm not gonna dig up a fossil just for you to understand something you'll never understand.

JUSTICE. I'm not asking you to dig it up. You don't have to talk about it. Just here if you want to. Like when you drove me to that hospital in Fort Worth. I was grateful for that. So I'm here to take you in, if you want to go in. No, not *take you in*, I said that wrong. I meant into the – into the, just into the…the, into the, yeah. You don't have to. You don't have to do anything. Jesus, Lot. Every single word is a whole galaxy. And I'm so bad at it. I'll shut up.

   (Pause.)

LOT. Yeah well school wasn't right for me anyway. Always getting kicked out the normal classes, getting stuck on an idea that didn't make sense to anyone but me. So I just stopped going. Then I was just around all day, in the old house. My dad was so mad at me. Couldn't keep up with the guys at the construction company. Body like a stick. Sticking around mother all day. A nuisance. Nothing to do. Then they were trying the special class, it was new, it was an experiment. Special needs. And was I one of them? Dad said this is your last chance. And the teacher liked me. Said I taught *her* things. But then after what happened with that girl, she had to kick me out. No choice. But I didn't do anything.

JUSTICE. I believe you.

LOT. I got confused.

JUSTICE. I believe you.

LOT. She couldn't talk or walk. She was in that class with me. She couldn't talk but I understood her. And I thought I loved her. Said those words to her. She wrote them back to me. Drew a picture to say it twice. She was an artist. She wanted to go into the lake with me. She wanted me to carry her in. We said let's do it naked – we would write about it, to each other, with pictures. Like a comic book telling our future. And it wasn't anything. I don't know – and even if it was something, it's what she wanted. It's what we both wanted. And we were kids. And we just wanted to do it, just go in, naked. That's all. And her mother and father thought it was more. They thought it was something it wasn't. They couldn't find her after school and then when they found her, they saw what they saw, and decided I was something awful. They called me trash. They made that word go on forever in me. They made me into something I wasn't. They called the, yeah, warthogs. The warthogs came and screamed at me. Took me in. Pushed me. Shoved me. I spent two nights there. And no matter what I said, no one believed me. And how's that for community. And I don't want to keep talking about this.

JUSTICE. Okay. Thank you for telling me.

   (Pause. Cautiously:)

Skinny-dipping is so fun. I'm glad you did that. I'm glad you loved her. You're a good man.

LOT. I don't care.

   (Long pause.)

JUSTICE. Listen, you're very very beautiful. Lot, you're the most beautiful guy. And I realized something recently. About the ghost I've been seeing. I don't think it's a dead man. I think it's a living man. I think it's you.

LOT. That's ridiculous.

JUSTICE. I think you're like some kinda time traveler.

LOT. No you don't.

JUSTICE. Don't tell me what I do or don't think.

LOT. Yes, okay.

JUSTICE. I think you've been building something incredible here. Something you need to be building – something for yourself – and God – something called art, yeah, but also a time machine, something that can stop the linear progression – something that breaks all the rules and brings us back to ourselves and keeps everyone connected to the invisible world.

LOT. Okay. Thank you for the sermonizing.

JUSTICE. What? I wasn't trying to sermonize.

LOT. I hate sermonizing. No word of God but the silent word. Nothing coming down, only going up. Just leave.

JUSTICE. See, why'd you have to switch like that? That hurt my feelings. I'm right here with you, just listening and responding, not trying to bend anything.

LOT. You're confusing me! You were doing it again! You're telling me I'm a ghost with these magic powers but I'm not a ghost, I'm right here and I never agreed to that!

JUSTICE. Okay. Okay. Damnit. You're right. Forget it. I'm sorry.

(Pause.)

Well this is – Jesus, this is as scary as it gets, but I think I gotta say that I love you.

LOT. Don't say that.

JUSTICE. I will say it. I love you.

LOT. Just don't say the word.

JUSTICE. You can't stop me from saying the word.

LOT. It hurts me.

JUSTICE. Okay I like you then. I like you.

LOT. What does that mean?

JUSTICE. It means that I like you. I always have.

LOT. What does that even mean?

JUSTICE. It means that I have a crush on you.

> *(Pause.)*

LOT. I don't know what any of that means.

JUSTICE. Well I don't either. I have no idea what it means. Just that I feel you with me all the time. And when I go to sleep I wish I were holding you. That's what that is.

LOT. You can't like me.

JUSTICE. Says who?

LOT. Says everything. You're normal and I'm fucked.

JUSTICE. No you're not.

LOT. Yes I am.

JUSTICE. Well then so am I. Yeah, so am I. I yearn for you, man. How embarrassing. How weird. How do you feel about that?

LOT. I feel fine about it.

JUSTICE. Yeah?

LOT. I guess so. I have no idea what it means. But I know what you said. And I know that I understand – yeah I understand. And I understand and I know what it is and I understand and I feel it too.

JUSTICE. You do?

LOT. Well I just want to tell you that I don't need you.

JUSTICE. Okay.

LOT. Yeah I don't need you. But I do want you.

JUSTICE. Oh. Okay. Really? Well I – haha, wow.

>　　*(They sit in silence for a bit and get nervous and then happy. And then nervous.)*

LOT. Well now I'm nervous.

JUSTICE. Me too. Is this real?

LOT. Don't ask me.

JUSTICE. Okay. You're weird.

LOT. So are you.

JUSTICE. Can you give me a hug?

>　　*(He approaches her slowly and gives her a hug. Then he pulls away.)*

LOT. I should most likely be alone now. And figure this out. Might take a long time.

JUSTICE. Okay, sure. I'll leave, yeah. We'll just... okay. Okay. Okay. But do we – okay. I mean I'm gonna need – no, not need. Okay. But – oh.

>　　*(She gets the tape recorder out of her purse.)*

I want you to know that Ginny wrote a song. Well, the lyrics to a song. She spoke them. And she'd like you to write the music to it. If you like. If you like – just let me know. If you listen to it and if you like the wavelength she's on, you know...collaborate with her.

LOT. This again.

JUSTICE. Yeah, this again. It's what she wants. I'm just the messenger. Up to you.

>　　*(**JUSTICE** tries to put the cassette tape in **LOT**'s hand. He keeps his fist clenched tight. She puts it on the ground and leaves.)*

(Now:)

*(**JUSTICE** and **CHRISTOPHER** with **GINNY**.
JUSTICE puts a tape in a boombox. The song
plays through the boombox.)*

LOT. *(Recorded.)* Alright, this is a version of it, I guess.
And hi, Ginny. And just give me a little more time, I
guess. I guess I love you, like a friend, and I suppose
that scared me. Okay. Sorry.

[MUSIC #5 – WHEN I SING TO MYSELF]

(He starts singing:)

NOBODY IS EVER GONNA HEAR THIS SONG
NOBODY WILL BE ALLOWED TO HEAR THIS SONG
CUZ I'M SINGING IT TO MYSELF AND YOU CAN'T HEAR IT
WHEN I SING TO MYSELF

IT'S OKAY THAT IT'S MESSY
WHEN I SING TO MYSELF.
I'M SINGING JUST ABOUT LOVE
WHEN I SING TO MYSELF.
BECAUSE THE TUNE I WROTE IS WHAT I WANT.
WHEN I SING TO MYSELF.
WHEN I SING TO MYSELF.

DON'T WANT NO ONE TO HEAR ME
SINGING WITH THE DOOR CLOSED.
WHEN I SING TO MYSELF
WHEN I SING TO MYSELF
I FORGET THAT I'M GROWN ON MY OWN ADVENTURE
AND SOMETIMES I FORGET THAT MY MOM PASSED AWAY.
AND SOMETIMES I REMEMBER.

*(**CHRISTOPHER** gets out a guitar and starts
playing it.)*

[MUSIC #6 – CHRISTOPHER FINALE PART ONE]

CHRISTOPHER. *(Singing.)*
    SHE HELPED ME EV'RY DAY –

GINNY. Excuse me, Christopher? You don't play the guitar.

CHRISTOPHER. Oh yeah, I start taking lessons when I'm forty-five.

GINNY. Like time travel? I'm terrified. That's awesome.

CHRISTOPHER. *(Singing.)*
    SHE HELPED ME EV'RY DAY, BUT THEN I'D HELP HER
    SHE STILL HELPS ME EV'RY DAY, NOW I CAN'T HELP HER
    I BET SHE MESSED WITH OUR INTERNET
    TO MAKE US WAKE UP
    I THINK SHE SENT ME A LETTER
    I THINK I'LL MEET HER AGAIN
    OH WE'LL ALL KEEP MEETING EACH OTHER

[MUSIC #7 – GINNY FINALE PART ONE]

GINNY. *(Singing.)*
    SHE USED TO TELL ME WHAT TO DO
    I'D GET MAD AND STORM INTO MY ROOM
    WE'D STAY UP LATE LAUGHING ABOUT PRINCES
    SHE DROVE ME AROUND
    SHE LOVED TOO MANY ICE CREAMS

Now Christopher, you go:

[MUSIC #8 – CHRISTOPHER FINALE PART TWO]

CHRISTOPHER. *(Singing.)*
    OH MY DAD DIDN'T DIE
    HE COULDN'T FIND THE SUPERMAN GUY
    ON HIS SHELF OF SPECIAL THINGS
    WE LOOKED FOR IT ENDLESSLY
    BUT THAT'S OKAY BECAUSE WE TALKED ABOUT IT
    ACTUALLY NO WE DIDN'T TALK ABOUT IT
    BUT LOOKING FOR IT FELT LIKE TALKING ABOUT IT
    AND HALF OF ME IS HER, HALF OF ME IS HIM,
    HALF OF ME IS ME, HALF OF ME IS YOU

AND SOMETIMES I FORGET TO BE AN ADULT.
AND SOMETIMES I FORGET THAT MY MOM PASSED AWAY.
AND SOMETIMES I REMEMBER.

[MUSIC #9 – GINNY FINALE PART TWO]

GINNY. And now: *(Singing.)*
THIS IS THE MARIAH CAREY PART OF THE SONG
THIS IS THE WHITNEY HOUSTON PART OF THE SONG
THIS IS THE CARRIE UNDERWOOD
THIS IS THE SHAWN MENDES
THIS IS THE DIXIE CHICKS
I AM THE DIXIE CHICKS
I AM THE DIXIE CHICKS

Justice, you go:

(At some point, **LOT** *has quietly joined them.)*

[MUSIC #10 – JUSTICE FINALE]

JUSTICE. *(Singing.)*
A SONG IS A FAM'LY.
IT ESCAPES TO BEYOND YOU.
YOU GET SOMETHING YOU SURE WEREN'T LOOKING FOR.
YOU'LL BECOME NEXT TO NOTHING WHEN YOU WALK
    THROUGH THE DOOR
TO A PLACE WHERE YOU'VE NEVER BEEN BEFORE:
THE LAND OF THE DEAD,
THE LAND OF THE DEAD.
THEY RISE UP TO GUT YOU.
YOU LET THEM GUT YOU.
THEY'RE JUST ORDINARY FOLK, JUST LIKE YOU AND ME.
WORRIED 'BOUT BULLSHIT, FEEDIN' ON MYSTERY.
THEN YOU FIND A SHAPE.
AND THAT SHAPE BECOMES YOU.
AND THAT SHAPE IS CALLED A FAMILY.
AND THE SHAPE IS A SONG.
AND THE SONG IS A FAILING.
THIS SONG IS A FAILING. A FAMILY.

[MUSIC #11 – WHEN I SING TO MYSELF (REPRISE)]

LOT. *(Singing.)*
NOBODY IS EVER GONNA HEAR THIS SONG
NOBODY WILL BE ALLOWED TO HEAR THIS SONG
CUZ I'M SINGING IT TO MYSELF AND YOU CAN'T HEAR IT
WHEN I SING TO MYSELF
WHEN I SING TO MYSELF

[MUSIC #12 – ONE MORE THOUGHT FROM GINNY]

GINNY. *(Singing.)*
AND THERE'S ONLY ONE MORE THING THAT I WANT TO SAY
I WAS RIDING A GHOST, A PTERODACTYL GHOST
THROUGH EV'RYONE'S HOME
JUST TO LEAVE THEM SOME ICE CREAM
SAFE IN THEIR FREEZER. FAT-FREE AND DAIRY-FREE.
JUST LIKE WHEN OPRAH GAVE EVERYONE CARS
BUT IT'S ME, A PTERODACTYL, AND OUR ICE CREAM
LEGOLAS IS WITH ME, MY HUSBAND IN THE STORY
FROM THE BOOK AND THE MOVIE, WE SAVE THE WORLD.

ALL. *(Singing.)*
NOBODY IS EVER GONNA HEAR THIS SONG
NOBODY WILL BE ALLOWED TO HEAR THIS SONG
CUZ I'M SINGING IT TO MYSELF AND YOU CAN'T HEAR IT

GINNY. *(Singing.)*
IN MY HOUSE IN CORSICANA
IN MY ROOM IN CORSICANA
IN MY BODY IN CORSICANA, TEXAS

(They've found themselves in an unforced circle. There's a pause after the song ends. **GINNY** *looks at* **LOT**.*)*

The End